I0659371

OLD MONEY

THE EVERETT BROTHERS SERIES
BOOK ONE

T.D. COLBERT

OLD MONEY

THE EVERETT BROTHERS SERIES, Book One

Copyright © 2025 T.D. Colbert

All rights reserved. No part of this book may be reproduced or transmitted in any form, including electronic or mechanical, without written permission from the publisher, except in the case of brief quotations in reviews. This book is a work of fiction. Names, characters, numerous places, and incidents are the product of the author's imagination, or are used fictitiously. This book may not be resold or given away in any manner.

Published: T.D. Colbert 2025

ISBN: 978-1-7352169-8-0

www.tdcolbert.com

Cover Design: Cosmic Letterz

Editing: Jenn Lockwood Editing

To everyone trying to find the light right now.
Look in the mirror - you are a part of it.

A NOTE FROM THE AUTHOR

Trigger warning: Mass shooting, violence.

According to Everytown, 125 people in the U.S. are killed by gun violence every day. Ending gun violence shouldn't be political. Visit www.everytown.org for more information.

SAWYER

"I'm fine, Mom," I sigh into the phone as I turn the corner on Helena Street. She still makes me call her every time I leave the mini-mart. Doesn't matter if it's a late shift, a morning shift, or anything in between. It's about a mile walk through a few neighborhoods back to campus, and she hates that I have to walk alone. I've pointed out to her that she is clear across the country from me, and if anything were to happen, there is quite literally nothing she would be able to do about it. But a mother's job is never done.

It's chilly for September, but I love it because it reminds me of home. I miss Seattle, and I miss my mom. But when the weather starts to turn here in New England, it gives me a little bit of that peace I feel when I'm there with her.

"I just hate that you have to work so much," she says, which is funny coming from her, because she's currently finishing up her shift at her first job at a coffee shop before she heads over to the diner she works at.

"Mom, it's *fine*. I like working. I can pay for all my books and things from this job.

Between that and the scholarship, I'll have almost no debt when I graduate. We've been through this. I'm *fine*. I still get to have fun. I still get to be a college kid. I am happy. I promise you," I say. It is mostly true, other than the unbearable amounts of stress I feel at basically all times. But she can't do anything about it, so there is no use in putting it on her too. She sighs again.

"I love you, baby," she says. I smile.

"I love you too, Mom. I can see my dorm from here. I'm almost back," I reassure her.

"Almost is not good enough," she says.

"Mom," I laugh, "it's 3:30 in the afternoon. The sun is shining. People are everywhere. I'm fine. Just stepped foot on campus."

She sighs.

"Fine," she moans. "I love you. Call me later."

As I'm rounding the corner toward the main hall, I see a figure out of the corner of my eye. As our paths draw closer, he turns his head slightly, and I can see his eyes within his hood. He has a large coat on, and it's zipped up. He's clutching his stomach, as if he's holding something.

My breath catches in my throat. That feeling builds in my stomach—the one where your body knows something is wrong before your brain does.

Stop. Go back.

Our eyes meet, and my feet freeze. I break our gaze and look out at the people in the quad, playing frisbee, studying, listening to music.

And then I see him unzip his coat.

And out it comes.

Hard, cold, metal death in his hands.

His eyes are on me before he looks away for a brief second, firing one round into the air.

I hear it before my brain registers what it is.

Then I hear the hums of death as it pours bullets out. And then, I hear the screams. I'm frozen in place for what feels like eternity as his eyes find mine again. Out of the corner of my eye, a tall, slender kid who I recognize from the gym is running in my direction.

"Run!" he's screaming, but then the bullets tear through him, hot blood spewing from his body in all directions as he tumbles to the ground, ten feet in front of me.

And then everything clicks.

SAWYER

I turn to run, getting knocked around by the hundreds of other people who have now realized what's happening. My purse flies out of my hand, but I keep running. I can't feel anything as my body moves on pure adrenaline. I'm not thinking. I'm just running. I turn down an alleyway on the back-side of campus between two buildings where some of the staff park. The steady humming is so loud bouncing off all the buildings that I can't tell which direction it's coming from. I turn back to a shriek behind me, and as I turn forward again, I see three men getting out of a black SUV, walking toward campus.

"Stop!" I scream as I run toward them. "Go back! He has a gun! Get back in the car! You have to go!" I shout. As I'm stepping off the curb toward them, I miss it, crashing into the pavement, sending my phone sliding across the parking lot and underneath a parked car. Behind me, shots ring out again, and I feel two hands pull me up.

"Come on," the man in front says. "Come with us. We will get you out of here."

I don't have the opportunity to survey the situation here. My choices are a maniac with a machine gun or a car full of strange men.

I take his hand and let him help me into the SUV. The other men get into the front, and the car peels out of the spot and off campus.

"To the city," the man in the back with me says, and the driver nods. I have no idea where I'm going or who I'm with. I have no way to contact anyone. I have no idea how many of my friends, my professors—anyone on campus, for that matter—are dead or alive.

My body starts to shake. I'm not crying. I'm not screaming. I'm not speaking. I'm just shaking.

I feel a hand reach across and take mine, and I turn to him. It's the first moment I've had to really look at him. He seems to be the man in charge. Not the most opportune moment to notice, but he's beautiful. He has dark-brown hair that's speckled with gray, with a matching beard and slight wrinkles around his eyes that make him look distinguished. But his eyes themselves, big and chestnut, have something soft about them. He feels familiar, but I don't have any brain power left to dedicate to figuring out why.

"Hey," he whispers as his grip tightens on my hand, "what's your name?"

"Uh, it's Sawyer," I stammer.

"Sawyer," he says, his eyes and his hand never leaving me. "My name is Julian. Can you look at me?"

I raise my eyes from our interlocked hands to his. Julian. Why do I know that name?

"You're safe. I'm going to bring you to my apartment in the city, okay? We will figure out what to do next from there. We will just take this one step at a time. Alright?"

I nod, clenching onto his hand. I have no idea how much time has passed, but before I know it, I'm in the middle of New York City. Campus is only about an hour away in Connecticut, and on the very rare occasion, I've made my way into Manhattan a few times with some friends.

God, my friends. I hope they're alive.

I reach my free hand down to my pocket, patting my pants on either side. I look up at him.

"I...I lost my phone. Oh, God. My mom... I lost my phone."

"It's okay," he says, squeezing my hand. "It's alright. We're about to be at my building. Let's go upstairs, and you can call her once we're out of the elevator." The two men open our doors, and the one on my side leads me around the car to where Julian is waiting for me. He takes my hand again, and one of the men scans a badge to let us into the building. We walk down a small hallway to an elevator that reads *Penthouse*, and he scans the badge again, then again once we get inside.

I can't move. It feels like an elephant is sitting on my chest, and my feet feel like they're made of cement. Finally, as we zip past all the other floors, the doors open.

"Come on, Sawyer," Julian whispers, leading me out and into a palatial penthouse suite. It's the most beautiful apartment I've ever seen, with the most amazing view, but I can't even begin to take anything in. I just stand there.

"Mr. Everett, the phone is for you, sir," one of the men says, and then it hits me.

Everett.

Julian Everett, of Everett Enterprises.

As in, one of the heirs to the multi-billion-dollar Everett Enterprises empire. As in, everything in this room is worth more than I am. Julian takes the phone.

"Hello, yes, we're safe," he says. "No, please don't reach out to the press. No. No one needs to know I was on campus. Yes. No. This isn't about me. Do they have any information? Jesus. Okay, thank you," he says, hanging up. He walks toward me.

"There's no information yet. Campus is locked down, but the gunman is still at large. Here, call your mom, and let her know you're safe. Then if it's okay, I'm going to have a doctor come up to take a look at you. I think you might need stitches."

He nods toward my head, and I reach a hand up to feel the wet, sticky blood on the side of my face. I hiss when I touch the gash just below my hairline. I'm not even sure what it's from—bumping into people or falling. I nod, taking the phone.

"Come," he says, ushering me farther into the apartment. "You can use the study." I follow him into a massive office with floor-to-ceiling built-ins, a huge desk, and an even bigger view. "I'll wait outside."

I wait till he closes the door then shakily dial my mom's number. She never used to answer strange numbers, but ever since I moved across the country, she answers everything.

"Hello, this is Emily Willis," she says, her voice shaky, and I can tell she's crying.

"Mom, it's me," I say, and I hear her bark out a sob.

"Oh, my god," she cries. "Oh, God. Oh, thank you, God," she says, and for a moment, it's just the two of us sitting on the phone, crying. "Tell me what happened, baby. Where were you? What did you see?"

I wipe my tears on my jacket sleeve and sniff.

"It...it happened right after I hung up with you. I saw him, Mom," I say. "I saw..." My voice trails off, and I can't stop crying.

"Oh, baby," she says. "I'm coming. I know there are some bad storms right now, but I'll get on the next flight—"

"No, Mom," I say, "you can't miss your shifts. It's okay. I'm okay."

"I'm coming, Sawyer. You're not being alone right now." I want to fight her on it. I know how badly she needs every penny she works for. But right now, the

8

only thing I want is a warm hug from my mom. "Where are you, baby?"

"I...uh... Mom, I think I'm in Julian Everett's apartment."

"What? Everett? Like *the* Everetts?"

"I...don't even know...I'm not even sure..." I start to say. Words aren't coming to me. Nothing is making any sense.

"Sweetheart, I think you're in shock. Who are you with? Let me talk to someone. Whose phone is this?"

As if he heard me, there's a short tap on the door before he opens it again.

"Everything okay?" he whispers. I nod.

"She wants to talk to you," I say. He nods, walking toward me.

"No problem," he says. He takes the phone. "Hello, this is Julian. Yes, hi. Yes, it's really me. Ma'am, I'm so sorry for the absolute terror you've probably been through over the last hour or so. Yes...well, yes. She saved me, actually. I was due for a speaking engagement on campus today, and she happened to be running as I was coming in. She stopped us...what's that? Yes."

As he's talking to her, I hear the ding of the elevator chiming through the apartment. One of the tall men who I presume to be Julian's security has poked his head into the room. Julian covers the speaker.

"Doc's here," he says. Julian nods toward me, and

the security man waves me out, leading me down the hall and up a set of stairs. We walk down the hallway, and to my left and my right, there is a door on either side. He takes me to the left and opens one of the doors. Inside is a massive suite, and he walks me through it to the extra-large bathroom.

"Sawyer, this is Dr. Simon," he says, holding his hand out to a young red-headed man who is opening a medical kit and setting things neatly on the massive bathroom vanity. "And I am Tyler, by the way. Other big guy downstairs is Russ. Holler if you need anything." I nod.

"Thank you," I say. I turn to Dr. Simon, who I would guess is fresh out of medical school. He doesn't look much older than me, but there's something really calming and commanding about his presence that puts me at ease.

"Sawyer, right?" he says. I nod, and he extends a hand to me. "It's nice to meet you, but I'm so sorry that it's under these circumstances. I'm so glad you're safe physically, but I know there is a long road ahead."

I nod.

The gunman hasn't even been apprehended.

"Mind if I take a look?" he asks, pointing to my head. He pats the toilet lid, and I sit down, closing my eyes. "Do you know what happened?" he asks. I clear my throat.

"I got bumped into when a bunch of us were running," I say, "and I also fell in the parking lot. I don't remember hitting my head, so I'm not sure which it was." He nods.

"Well, either way, we will get you cleaned up," he says. There's a knock on the door just as he's reaching for some gauze and something to sterilize and clean the cut. Julian steps in.

"How's she looking, Doc?" he asks.

"Hey, Julian," he says without taking his eyes off what he's doing. "She looks good, considering. Three, maybe four stitches and she should be good to go."

Julian nods and then sits on the edge of the free-standing tub that's in front of the toilet.

"So, I talked to your mom," he says, "explained how you ended up here. There are some flight delays coming out of Seattle right now because of weather, but she will be on the next commercial one they can get out of there. Unfortunately, none of our jets are on the West Coast right now, so we can't get her here any sooner than that. She's on standby until my people can get her a ticket."

"But...how...she can't..." I start to ask, but when we make eye contact, I know why. He's paying for it. "You don't have to...that's so nice of you." He nods and keeps talking.

"We've ordered you a new phone that should be here shortly, and I have one of my guys working on downloading your contacts so you can start checking in with your friends."

We make eye contact again, and I swallow as Dr.

Simon jabs me with the needle of Novocaine. I wince, and I feel Julian's hand on mine.

"No updates on the shooter as of now, but I do know that campus is locked down with no one allowed on or off until law enforcement catches him. I spoke with your mom, and I'm happy to put you up in a hotel, but you are also more than welcome to stay here tonight. You can have this suite. It locks completely from the inside, if that makes you feel any more comfortable. She wasn't a fan of the idea of you being alone tonight, and I don't think she's wrong. Obviously, it's up to you, but I wanted to let you know that you are more than welcome to stay put."

I swallow as Dr. Simon prepares the stitches while the Novocaine sets in. I clear my throat.

"Thank you," is all I can muster, my voice cracking. He squeezes my hand.

"I'm going to go check on the status of your phone," he says. I nod as our hands break from each other.

A little while later, Dr. Simon is cleaning up his supplies, and we're headed back downstairs. He and Julian talk for a few minutes, and then I see Julian hand him an envelope as Russ walks him to the elevator. Tyler is nowhere to be seen, and suddenly, I'm aware that it's just me and the random billionaire who swept me up to his tall tower today.

There are three large brown bags on the massive kitchen island, and Julian grabs them, walking toward me. There are three huge couches in the middle of the sunken living room centered around a large fireplace.

"Before you sit," he says—not that I was going to —"I thought you might want to change. I guessed on sizes, but one of my assistants grabbed a few things in a few different sizes so you could wear whatever was the most comfortable. I thought you might want to... get the day off of you."

One thing about me is that I *hate* to feel like I owe people. Gifts make me uncomfortable because I have this overwhelming sense that I'm only worthy of them if I can return the favor. But today, I can't seem to care. And he's right. I want nothing more than to get this outfit off of me. I want to burn it.

"Thank you," I say.

"There is shampoo and soap and everything you should need in the bathroom in your suite. If you need anything else, I'll be right down here. The phone should get here by the time you're done."

I nod and go back upstairs. I choose an ultra-soft sweatsuit and some fluffy socks from the bag and get into the shower, turning the water as hot as it will go. And while the room fills with steam, I sob quietly against the glass.

I get myself together, wash my hair and body, and get dressed. When I get back downstairs, Julian is plugging a phone into one of the chargers that has magically appeared from one of the arms of the couch.

"Just in time," he says. "Aaron said that he was able to get into your cloud and download your contacts. He is still working on getting your pictures, but the contacts are here." He hands me the phone. "Do you want some privacy?"

I think about it for a moment.

"No," I say. "Could you sit with me?"

He nods, grabbing a glass of whiskey off the table and scooting closer to me.

"Of course."

JULIAN

I'm trying to stay as calm as I can. I watch as she opens her contacts, her fingers shaking as she types in the first name. "Lucy" flashes on the screen. It rings a few times, but no answer. Someone named Maddie is next, but she doesn't answer either. Spencer is next, and while his call goes directly to voicemail, he texts her back immediately.

"He's okay," she breathes. "He is locked in the arts building with his graphic design class. They've been in there for three hours," she reads. "He's talked to a few of my other friends too."

I see her scroll back through her texts, sending some off to the people who didn't answer. She stares down at the screen for a few moments, willing it to light up, but it doesn't. Finally, I put my hand on top of the phone.

"Hey," I say, and she looks up at me. "It doesn't

mean they're not alive. Phones could be dead, cell towers down...there are no answers yet."

I'm trying like hell to sound convincing. Statistically, her friends are most likely alive. Carrington University is a tiny little school in Connecticut that has gotten the reputation over the last few years of being almost as hard to get into as the Ivy Leagues. It's small, but out of twenty thousand kids, statistically, her friends are hopefully okay.

"Hungry?" I ask. She's been with me for hours, and she hasn't even mentioned food. She shrugs.

"Not really," she says. I know I should encourage her to eat, but I'm letting her set the pace right now. I want to ask her questions: figure out how she ended up on the East Coast, figure out why she ended up at Carrington, learn more about her. She's a tiny little thing, her short black hair tied up in a knot on her head, her dark-green eyes streaked and bloodshot. "Is there any news on flights yet?"

I shake my head.

"Not yet," I say. "But my people are on it. Checking in on the hour, every hour, until we can get her on a plane."

She nods.

"Thank you, Julian," she says, biting her bottom lip. "For all of this."

I lean forward, putting my hand on hers again.

"Thank *you*, Sawyer," I say. "Did you decide where you want to stay?"

She clears her throat and tucks a stray curl behind her ear.

"If it's okay with you, I'll just stay here," she says. I nod, fighting a smile. I was hoping she'd say that. I want to keep an eye on her, although I don't really know why.

"Of course," I say. "The suite is yours." She smiles and nods.

"I think I'm going to try to sleep," she says, standing slowly from the couch. I stand with her.

"Of course," I say again. "If you need anything at all, I'm the door down the hall. Help yourself to anything in the kitchen you want, anytime you want. And Sawyer?"

Her big eyes look up to me.

"I'm right here, okay? You're not alone."

She smiles slightly and nods then heads for the stairs.

I'VE BEEN LYING in my bed for about two hours now, staring out at the city. I haven't had much time to do my own processing because I've been so distracted by Sawyer's. The adrenaline has kicked in again, making me wired and jumpy. If I had stepped onto that campus just a few moments earlier or a few moments later...who knows. That might have been it for me. I check my phone every few minutes, seeing if Tierra was able to make Emily's reservation, but nothing.

And then I hear a loud crash from down the hall,

and I'm on my feet in a moment, heart racing. I knock on her door and wait a beat, but there's no response. I turn the handle and find that she didn't lock it. When I open it, I see her crouching down on the ground, picking up pieces of a broken vase. The light from the hallway hits her perfectly, and I see the tears in her eyes and streaming down her cheeks.

"I'm so sorry if I woke you," she says, trying to steady her voice. "I was trying to get to the bathroom, but I ran into the dresser and knocked the vase off. I'm sorry. I'll get this cleaned up—" she says, looking down at the mess. I walk across the room slowly so I don't scare her, and when I reach her, I bend down and grab her wrists. I pull her gently to her feet and lead her a few steps away from the glass. I look down at her for a moment, and then I pull her into my chest. I cradle her head against my bare skin, and I feel her arms snake around my body as she finally gives in. She sobs into me, her tears streaming down my stomach. We stand like this for what feels like hours but, in reality, is only a few minutes. When she's calmed down some, I get her some tissues from the bathroom and lead her to the bed. I pat it for her to sit down, and then I clean up the glass and flowers and blot the water up with a towel.

She's still sitting as still as a statue when I walk over to the bedside and grab the remote from the nightstand. I turn on the TV and look at her.

"When I was a kid, this is what I'd watch with my grandfather when I couldn't sleep," I tell her. I turn on episode one of *Cheers,* and I let the bright colors and warming theme song fill the room. Then I pull the armchair next to the bed closer to it. "Is it okay if I stay in here and watch with you for a bit?"

She nods, looking up at me through puffy eyes, the tears still gleaming on her face. I scoot closer to her then turn the volume up some and put my feet up on the ottoman. She slides her hand farther across the bed in my direction, leaving it at the edge, and without saying anything, I put mine on hers. As soon as I do, I feel her clutch onto me. She doesn't need words right now. She just needs to know someone is there. And that's going to be me. After a few minutes, she finally drifts off to sleep. I lean forward, careful not to move our hands and disturb her, getting slightly closer to her. I stroke her hair gently, staring at her, wondering all there is to know about this beautiful young woman in front of me.

I don't know anything about her, but I do know that I'd do anything to take away the stain that this day will leave on the rest of her life.

SAWYER

*W*hen I wake up, it takes me a moment to remember everything that happened. For a moment, I have peace. I'm staring out over the upper west side, looking down at Central Park and the city that never seems fazed. But when I see my new phone on the nightstand next to me, I remember where I am and why I'm here, and that sinking feeling returns to the pit of my stomach.

I slink out of the bed and let my feet hit the floor, making my way out the door and down the stairs. I can hear Julian on the phone.

"No. No, I don't want anyone to know I was there. No, this isn't about me. There are people—college kids —dead. This doesn't need to be the Everett show. Yes. Just find out who they all were, and make an anonymous donation to cover all the funeral costs. Yes. All of them. No. Yes, okay."

College kids dead. And he's paying for the funerals. The pit grows deeper in my belly.

When I get to the main level, I see a woman in the kitchen, putting out platters of food, Russ and Tyler are near the elevator, and Julian is still talking, pacing the apartment. When he sees me, he smiles.

He hangs up and makes his way toward me as I reach the bottom of the stairs. I look up at him, and for a moment, I feel a little lighter. His dark waves are styled immaculately, and he's wearing a shirt and tie that would normally make me feel a little weak in the knees.

If it weren't for the circumstances that brought me to him, these last sixteen hours or so would have me absolutely salivating over him.

"Good morning," he says.

"Good morning," I say back.

"Bonnie is in the kitchen, whipping up a few things. I wasn't sure what you liked, so she's made a few different dishes." I nod. Something she's making smells delicious, and suddenly, I'm very aware that I haven't eaten in almost a full twenty-four hours. "I have to go, but Russ is going to take you to the airport. Your mom's flight gets in in about an hour."

That's the best news I've heard in...well...sixteen hours.

"Oh my gosh," I say, "thank you so much."

"We reserved a suite for the two of you in the city for as long as you need." My eyes widen.

"Julian, you've done enough," I say. His eyebrows

knit together as he stares down at the ground, then he lifts his eyes to me.

"No one should have to go through what you're going through, Sawyer," he whispers, and I swallow the lump in my throat. "Campus is still locked down," he says. I swallow again, but it's getting harder.

"Is there...has there been any..." My voice trails off.

"Thirty-three students and staff members were killed," he whispers. "The gunman...he killed himself in the middle of the quad. Police are still searching campus for students and staff who were locked down and didn't get word of the all-clear. They're also still searching for...victims. So far, classes are canceled for the next week."

I bite my lip, then I look down at my phone. No new messages.

"I'm so sorry I have to go," he says as he steps toward me. I force a smile and wave him off.

"Please," I say, "you have done so much for me. You don't owe us any of this, seriously."

He reaches out and gently takes my hand in his.

"Please stop saying that, Sawyer. Please," he says. I swallow again. "Have something to eat, and then go get your mom. I'll be in touch."

I smile faintly back at him, but as he turns away, I feel myself reach out and grab his hand. He freezes, looking down at them for a moment, then our eyes meet again before he walks to the elevator with Tyler behind.

· · ·

AN HOUR LATER, I'm waiting anxiously at the gate at JFK for my mom's flight. I've tracked it every five seconds, watching the flight number pop up on the screens over and over again. And then finally, when I see her walking through, I melt. I run to her and let myself become a puddle again while she holds me. I take in her familiar touch, her smell, the way she cradles me like I'm a baby.

I don't care who is around. I don't care who's watching. I just care that my mom is here.

Finally, I get it together enough that we walk out the doors toward the car. Tyler is behind us, carrying her bag, and he opens the door for us. I don't have anything of my own, just a bag packed with the clothes that Julian bought me.

My mom and I hold hands the entire way from the airport to the hotel.

We get to the hotel, and Tyler walks us in and checks us in at the desk. We say our goodbyes, and then Mom and I go up to our suite—another pent-house, I might add—change into the robes, and lie in bed, watching movies. She scratches my head as I lie in her lap.

"I can't believe he paid for us to stay here," she says. "He's so kind."

I sigh.

"I know. I feel so guilty about it," I say.

"I know, honey. But I would have done anything to get here as fast as possible."

. . .

23

My phone has pinged sporadically all day. Spencer is with his parents back in New Hampshire. He knows that the rugby team also made it, because they were off campus at a match.

Maddie called me around noon. She had been locked in a weight room with some of her friends for six hours before the police came to clear them. She's back in New Jersey with her family. But there's one more thing.

She heard that the gunman had gone into Lex Hall. My dorm. Where I live with Lucy.

Lucy.

Maddie hasn't heard from her either.

We tell each other we love each other. We say our goodbyes.

I hang up the phone, and then I collapse back on the bed, tears endlessly streaming down my face.

I don't know, but I do know.

I'm never going to see her again.

JULIAN

*I*t's been three days since Tyler dropped Sawyer and her mom at the hotel. And it's been three minutes since I've last thought about her.

On the outside, she looked and seemed so helpless. Nothing to her name. Completely traumatized.

But then when I spoke to her mom, I realized how fucking tough she was. She was going to go through one of the biggest mass murder events in recent history and carry on with life as usual. She told her mom not to come because she knew she couldn't afford it. She didn't have her purse, her wallet, her phone, but she told me not to pay for anything.

And it made me want to do it all that much more.

I check in with my contact at the university a few times a day. Being that I'm the school's biggest donor, I get a lot of perks. I also ask that he makes sure it does not get out that I was on campus.

All the victims have been identified. He's sending me the list.

And as I scroll through it, I see the name.

Lucy.

I know there are probably multiple Lucies at Carrington, so I ask him to check who her roommate was.

Sawyer Willis.

Fuck.

I sigh in the backseat of the car, swiping a hand down my face.

I open the contact for her phone and send a text.

Checking in on you. It's been a few days.

I see the dots pop up, then disappear, then pop up again.

It's Julian, by the way, I send back. *Took the liberty of adding my number to your phone, in case you need anything.*

Thank you so much, she sends back. *Lucy is dead.*

I know. I'm so sorry, Sawyer.

Dots, then no dots. Then dots again.

My mom has to go back tomorrow.

I know. A car will pick you guys up to bring her to the airport tomorrow around eight.

You don't have to do that.

Stop, Sawyer. Keep my number. Text if you need anything. Anytime.

. . .

THE NEXT MORNING, as Tyler is getting ready to take the elevator down to the car, I stop him.

"I'm riding with you," I say. He gives me a confused look. "I want to meet her mom. Check in on them." He nods without questioning me, and we go down to the car.

When we pull up outside of their hotel, I reach for the door.

"I'll get them, J," Tyler says. "You'll be spotted here."

He's not wrong. We got them a suite in the Grand Hyatt right above Grand Central Station. We just pulled up in a blacked-out Escalade. Eyes are already on us. And it's not like I'm not used to being noticed, and normally, I don't let it faze me. But right now, it does, because I'd be drawing them to her. Not only do I not want to do that to her and her mom, but I also don't want anything connecting me back to that campus. I can see the headlines now, the requests for interviews.

Billionaire escapes mass shooting.

Julian Everett narrowly escapes gunman.

No.

Thirty-three people are dead.

So as much as the chivalry in me is dying to get out, I let Tyler greet them and get the door.

And when Sawyer sees me, I see her eyes widen and her shoulders instantly loosen.

"H-hi," she says with a faint smile.

"Hi, Sawyer," I say as she climbs in, scooting to the back of the SUV.

"You're here," she says, just above a whisper. I smile.

"I am," I say. "I wanted to check in on you. And meet you, Emily."

Emily climbs in and takes the seat next to me as I stick my hand out to her.

"Oh, my gosh, Mr. Everett. It is—"

"Julian, please," I say, cutting her off. She smiles, and then I see tears in her eyes. She springs across the seat, pulling me in for a long hug. Her perfume smells delicious, and this might be one of the best hugs I've ever gotten. I let her sit for a moment, feeling her body move up and down with little sobs.

"Okay, Mom," Sawyer says, "let him breathe." I chuckle as Emily lets me go and sits back in her seat.

"I'm sorry," she says, wiping her eyes as Tyler pulls the car out. "I just... I'm so grateful that you were there when you were. You're like...you're like her guardian angel. You will never know how thankful I am."

Sawyer looks down at her hands and clears her throat as I look back at her.

"No, ma'am," I say. "She was *my* guardian angel."

Her eyes lift to mine, and they lock for a moment.

The rest of the ride, Emily is peppering Sawyer with questions. What will she do until classes start back? Is she sure she doesn't want to come home with her? Is she sure she'll be alright?

"Emily," I say, interjecting just as we are pulling

into the airport, "I promise you that I will stay in touch with her. She's not alone over here on the East Coast—I promise you that."

I look back at her and wink as I reach out and squeeze Emily's hand.

I don't know why I feel responsible for her, but it's more than that. I also *want* to be there for Sawyer. I want to know she's okay.

"Thank you," Emily whispers as Tyler opens her door. Sawyer scoots out of the car, and Tyler closes the door to give them some privacy as they say their goodbyes.

"I'll see you over Thanksgiving?" Emily says. Sawyer nods. They hug one last time, both wiping tears, and then Tyler opens the door again for Sawyer. And as we drive away, I reach over and squeeze her hand.

"Have you been in touch with any of your friends any more?" I ask cautiously. I know it's obviously a sensitive subject.

She nods.

"There's a vigil on campus in a few weeks," she says. "A few of us are supposed to be going together."

I nod.

"That'll be good for you to all be together," I tell her. There's a little bit of a silence, and then I tap her shoulder. "I meant what I said to your mother, Sawyer. You're not alone." Her eyes meet mine again, and she nods.

"Thank you, Julian," she whispers, although I

know that, right now, all she feels is probably alone. "They've canceled classes for the rest of the semester. Eight weeks of no classes to distract me. That'll be interesting."

I think for a moment.

I can think of a few things to keep her busy...

God, I'm a pig. What the fuck is wrong with me? She's sad and vulnerable and alone—no. She might be sad and vulnerable, but she won't be alone. I'll make sure of it.

"Did you have anything you wanted to do for the rest of the week?" I ask.

She laughs and shrugs. "I don't get out much," she says. "And things cost money. So I typically just lay low. Most of my friends are still with their families. We're not allowed back on campus until Saturday, so I was just going to hang at the hotel."

I nod again.

"Do you want to be alone?" I ask her.

She cocks an eyebrow. "As opposed to...?"

"As opposed to not being alone," I say with a half-smile.

She fights a smile and clears her throat. "I mean... don't you have, like...a few hundred businesses to run?"

I laugh. I pull my phone out of my pocket and dial Natasha.

"Hey, Nat," I say when she picks up. "Do me a favor. Can you rearrange some things today? Uh, actually, all of it. I need the day. Yep. That's fine. Thank you," I say, hanging up. Then I look over at her. "The few hundred businesses can wait."

JULIAN

"*J*ulian, I know what you told my mom, but you...you don't owe us—me— anything. You have already done so much more in the last few days than anyone would ever be expected to do for a complete stranger. Please, I can't handle feeling like there's this list of things I'll never be able to repay you for."

I lean closer to her and cover her hand with mine.

"If you hadn't stopped me from walking onto that campus, I might be dead. I think you keep forgetting that little piece of the puzzle. I'm not a man who needs to be repaid. But I am a man who sticks to his word. Okay?"

She swallows and thinks for a moment. Then she nods slowly.

"Okay," she whispers. I squeeze her hand before I look to Tyler.

"Ty, can you take us out to Bendmere?"

"You got it, boss," he says.

We ride quietly but not in an uncomfortable kind of way. I replay some of her words as we go. "Complete stranger" keeps ringing in my ears. It's true I've only known her for a total of about ninety-six hours. But "strangers" don't go through what we've already been through together. Strangers don't hold each other, share tears. I don't know what we are, but "strangers" doesn't quite cover it.

I've done a little of my own research on her, but I know there's more than what's going to show up in a quick internet search. And I want to know it all.

After about an hour, we're pulling into the tiny coastal town of Bendmere, which my family has made famous over the last century. Bendmere is where my great-grandfather built our family's estate, Bedell House, after the oil boom. Rivaling only the Rockefellers, Enzo Everett was the second richest man in the entire country. And as the bloodline went down, those fortunes only grew exponentially.

The thing I love about Bendmere is that because my family frequents it so much, the people who live here are largely unfazed by us when we do make our way into town.

"Bedell House?" Tyler asks through the rearview. I think about it for a moment, but I don't know who from my family may be at the property today. I didn't reserve it, and the last thing Sawyer needs is a run-in with any of the eccentric billionaires I call my family.

"Not today," I say. "You can just drop us off at the

boardwalk." Tyler nods in the mirror. Bendmere is the only place my family doesn't require a major security detail. Tyler will be close by, but we can have some privacy.

When he lets us out of the car, I lead her up onto the boardwalk. I have on a button-down and slacks, and I throw on a pair of sunglasses to at least play up some sort of disguise. She's wearing an oversized sweatshirt and leggings, and she looks fucking adorable.

We walk a little ways, letting the chilly salt air blow around us. The boardwalk is fairly empty because it's the off-season, so we have it largely to ourselves. We walk in and out of a few stores, and I watch her intently as she looks at things: some clothes, a bracelet, a candle, some coffee.

We get to a little Christmas shop, and she's turning a gold-plated ornament in her hand that reads *Bendmere*.

"You want that?" I ask. She scoffs and shakes her head.

"No, Julian," she says. "You're not helping much with the whole not-making-me-feel-like I-owe-you thing." She smiles as she walks out of the store, and I follow behind but not before I snag one of the ornaments and hand the shop owner a hundred-dollar bill.

I tuck it into my pocket. I'll figure out how to slip it to her later.

We walk around for a few more hours, eating pretzels, cotton candy, and a few other things that would make my trainer's head explode before we make our way to a bench. The sun is starting to go down, and she shivers as she wraps her sweatshirt around herself tighter.

"Can I take you to dinner?" I ask. She turns to me and bites her lip.

"Okay," she says.

A few minutes later, Tyler is dropping us off at one of my favorite spots here in town, a little Italian place called Mama Tilly's.

Tilly's granddaughter, Marni, owns it now and brings us to a little private table in the back. I see her eyeing Sawyer, and for a minute, it makes me uncomfortable. Not because I give a shit what she thinks about me walking in here with a girl who is significantly younger than me, but because my protective instincts kick in whenever Sawyer is concerned. But I let out a long breath when she hands us our menus and slips back into the kitchen. Bendmere and the people in it are good to us. They practice discretion.

I watch her read the menu, and then I order us a bottle of the house wine and some mozzarella sticks.

Finally, we order our entrees, a steak for me and ravioli for her, and then it's just the two of us.

"So," I say, taking a bite of my salad, "a full academic scholarship, huh? So you're real unintelligent, then."

She giggles as she takes a sip of her wine.

"Did some research, did you?" she asks. I shrug and smile.

"Maybe. Tell me more about the parts that I can't search," I say. She looks at me through narrowed eyes for a minute then lets out a sigh.

"Well, there's not much to tell. It's just me and my mom. My parents had me at eighteen, and my dad ditched when he found out she was pregnant," she says. "My grandparents kicked my mom out when she got pregnant, so it's always just been us. She works three jobs to pay the bills. She's the best person I know." Her voice cracks a little bit, but she keeps going. "I applied to every state school and a bunch of others on the West Coast, but I got a full ride for academics to Carrington, so Carrington it was. Plan is to get my degree, get a job back home, and make it so she can finally breathe."

I nod, hanging on every word she says.

"Full ride. Impressive. What is it that you want to do?" I ask.

"My degree will be in communications," she says. "I'm not sure yet. Just something that pays the bills." I nod. She takes a sip of wine, then she smiles. "You know, you're not the only one who did some research."

I raise an eyebrow and give her a half-smile as I take another sip of my wine.

"Oh yeah?" I ask. I hold my hand out. "Alright, then. Let's see what you've learned."

"Oldest of Cato Everett's three sons. You're next in line to run Everett Enterprises. You oversee most of the domestic businesses. Your youngest brother has a different mom than you and your middle brother. Your dad has a bit of a...reputation. Not super well-liked amongst people he employs. You are *not* the brother that dates all the models. You were engaged once about ten years ago, but it got called off," she says nervously. She waits a beat, then she says, "And you're thirty-seven."

The corner of my mouth tugs up again.

"I am," I say. "And you're twenty-two."

SAWYER

I'm chalking it up to the fact that this has been the most traumatic fever dream of a week ever, and that's why I haven't had a complete meltdown over the fact that I've been fully sponsored by one of the richest men on the fucking planet. Dinner felt so completely...normal. He doesn't *feel* rich, even when he's paying the bill, even when his security picks us up, even when he's spending thousands of dollars on a hotel suite for me like it's pocket change.

Which, I guess it is.

There was a strange calmness all day with him, so much so that there were multiple times when I forgot why we were together in the first place, numerous times that I forgot how we met. And that's what terrifies me about the fact that we're approaching the hotel. Because in a few short minutes, he will pull away, and for the first time since the shooting, I'll truly be alone.

I must have been in a daze, because I don't realize Tyler has parked outside the Hyatt until Julian says my name.

"Sawyer?" he says. "You okay?"

"Hmm, oh, yeah, sorry," I say with a nervous laugh. "Just tired. Thank you so much for today. Both of you," I say, looking at Tyler through the rearview mirror. He smiles before getting out to walk around to my door. As I'm scooting toward the door, I feel Julian grab my hand.

"Are you going to be okay tonight?" he asks. I force a smile and wave my hand.

"Oh, yeah. I'm so exhausted I'll probably fall right to sleep."

Lies.

He nods and gives me a sad smile back.

"Thank you, Julian," I say. "For everything."

He leans forward, and to my surprise, he leaves a soft kiss on my cheek. I get out as Tyler opens the door and wave as I walk through the revolving doors. I make it up to my room and lock the door just before the tears start to fall. But as I'm about to go full on sob-fest, my phone starts ringing. I clear my throat and take in a deep breath through my nose.

"Hey, Ma," I say. "Landed safe?" I force the chipper tone as she tells me about her flight and how Julian flew her first class again. She asks me what I did today, and I tell her.

"Oh, my goodness," she says. "He really is such a good man."

I smile.

"He is," I say.

"Are you okay, honey? Are you sure you don't want to come home for the semester? Do you want to stay on the phone with me until you fall asleep?"

"No, Ma," I say. "I need to stay here and work. And no, it's okay. I know you've gotta be beat. I am too. I'm okay. Really. Let me know when you get to the diner in the morning, please. I love you."

"I love you, baby. I can't wait to see you again."

"You too, Mama," I whisper as I hang up.

I change into the pajamas that Julian bought me and curl up in the bed that he paid for. The sheets are cold and unfamiliar on my skin. And then the tears come again. I clutch the pillow as they fall.

Falling for my mother and the fear she felt.

Falling for the thirty-three empty pillows tonight and every night.

Falling for the students like me who couldn't escape like I did, who were trapped for hours, wondering if they'd survive.

Falling for the professors and custodians, and cooks, and counselors who wondered if they'd see their families again.

And falling for me. Because I wasn't ready to die.

I jump when my phone vibrates next to me, and I freeze when I see Julian's name light up.

I sniff a few times, trying to get myself to sound more together before I answer.

"Hello?" I say just above a whisper.

"Check the desk," he says.

"Huh?"

"The desk in your room," he says. "I had a delivery come while we were out."

I sniff and scoot off the bed, walking toward the desk where a box sits. I open it to find a brand-new tablet.

"What is this?"

"Turn it on," he says. I do.

"You can set it up however you want to," he says, "but I did take the liberty of downloading a few things to it."

"What...what is this?"

"Check the downloads folder," he says. I tap it and up pops every episode of every season of *Cheers*. I smile to myself.

"Julian," I say, climbing back onto the bed.

"I'm starting season two, episode four right now. Put it on. We can watch it together until you fall asleep."

I don't know what's going on in the show at all, but I know two things: One, Ted Danson was a total babe. And two, I'm starting to think my mother was right. Maybe Julian is my guardian angel.

JULIAN

T've been in Chicago, D.C., Dallas, and Charlotte in the span of two weeks for work, but every single night, I've been in bed, on the phone with her. And I'm not even mad that she skipped a few episodes without me. I was supposed to stay in Charlotte another night, but I'm flying back to New York now. Tomorrow will be her first day back on campus. They're supposed to let the students go to the vigil then to their dorms to collect their things. Classes have been canceled until the start of the spring semester in January, but students have until Thanksgiving break to stay on campus.

Sawyer says she's staying as long as possible to "get a few extra shifts in" at the mini-mart before she flies home to her mom. I don't know why I feel the need to be closer to her, but I do. She hasn't asked me to be around. We haven't talked since last night when I heard the steady humming of her snores as she finally drifted off.

I click the tip of my pen up and down as Rachel talks, and she finally catches on.

"Julian?" she asks from the front of the board room.

"Hmm?" I say.

"Did you have a chance to look at the revenue reports?" she asks. I clear my throat and lean forward.

Okay, Julian. Time to get back into boss mode.

"I did, yes," I say. "I'm pleased with where things are. Projections have us up by 16% since this time last year."

She nods.

"Let's put some of that excess back into personnel. Figure out their bonuses, but let's also do an extra percentage increase in Q1."

She nods and smiles.

"You got it," she says, nodding to another woman who just started with Rachel a few months ago. Rachel is my right-hand woman. She's smart, dedicated, and loyal to a fault. She's been with the company almost as long as I have. In my opinion, she has one of the most important roles in the entirety of Everett Enterprises. She's the head of Human Resources. One of the biggest changes I've been trying to make since my father named me head of all the East Coast subsidiaries was to invest in the people.

I don't want to be one of those billionaires who walks around on streets of gold while the people who make us the money work three jobs to keep a roof over their heads.

People like Emily.

One of my biggest initiatives has been implementing a salary minimum. That no employee that works for us makes less than seventy-five thousand, regardless of what their job title is. While my father has approved it for a few of our smaller subsidiaries, it hasn't made its way across the board. My dad loves money. He loves his bottom line. He's old school. But I'm not giving up.

We finish up our meeting, I shake hands with my dad's board buddies, and then I'm getting in the car headed back to the jet.

By the time we land back in New York, it's already dark. I look at my watch. About an hour until the vigil. I had a car going to pick her up from the hotel to bring her back to campus. I pull out my phone.

You on the way? I send.

Yes. Thank you again for the ride.

Just landed back in NY. I know tonight will be tough. I'll be thinking about you.

Dots, then no dots, then dots.

Thank you, Julian.

I PUT my phone back in my pocket as Russ is pulling out of the airfield.

"Russ," I say, "let's head to Colby's. I want a sub." He looks at me through the mirror but just nods. I know what he's thinking. Why are we driving forty minutes outside the city to get a sub when I live in the middle of Manhattan and could get a sub on any corner? But luckily, Russ doesn't ask questions, and he has trained Tyler not to either.

But the answer is that Colby's is a sandwich place out in Connecticut—about fifteen minutes from the Carrington campus.

I check some emails, text my dad to let him know how the meetings went, and check in with my brothers. All is well with Everett Enterprises, so I'm clocking out for the night. But it doesn't stop me from scrolling through my texts every five minutes to see if anyone— any college student, in particular—has checked in.

I get my sandwich and eat it in the car while I peruse on my phone. The vigil should be over by now. I feel my stomach turn. She'll be going back to her dorm room soon. I wait a few more minutes, and then I let out a sigh.

Just as I'm about to tell Russ to start heading back to the city, my phone buzzes on the leather seat next to me. I reach for it frantically.

"Sawyer?" I answer.

"I can't do it," she sobs. "I...I tried to go in, but I can't do it. This is the last place she was alive. I don't... I can't..."

"Where are you?" I ask.

"I'm in the stairwell in my building," she says. I picture her curled in a ball all alone on those damn stairs. I should have gone with her.

"What building?" I ask, putting her on speaker so that Russ can hear.

"Lex Hall," she says. Russ nods in the mirror, plugging it into his GPS and peeling out of our parking spot.

"Just stay on the phone with me, Sawyer," I say. "I'm coming."

After breaking several traffic laws and ignoring several stop signs, Russ has us on campus in thirteen minutes.

"There aren't any spots, boss," he says. I look up, and there are still cop cars all along the perimeter of the lot.

"Just stop here," I say. He looks at me.

"Boss..."

"Just stop the car, Russ," I say. He does, and I jump out. "We'll be out in a second."

I run toward Lex Hall, waiting for a student to scan their badge and then jumping in behind them— which, in hindsight, probably isn't the best thing to do, considering this campus just had a very unwelcome visitor less than a week ago. But Sawyer needs me. I walk to the stairwell. "Which floor are you on?" I ask.

"Third."

JULIAN

I hang up the phone so she doesn't hear me huffing and puffing then take the stairs two by two until I get to the third floor. The hallways are filled with students and families, talking, hugging, crying. But she just sits in the corner of the stairwell, all by herself. I reach a hand out and pull her up off the ground then pull her into my chest. I don't know how to get past this feeling of never wanting to leave this girl by herself again. But every time I show up, it only gets stronger.

"Is there anything you need from your room?" I ask her once she's calmed down. I look around. No one has seemed to notice me yet, but I'd rather not wear out my welcome. She thinks for a minute.

"My laptop and maybe some clothes. Fuck," she says. "How am I going to do this? I need to be able to come back here." I put a hand on her shoulder.

"We'll figure it out. One step at a time," I say. "Give me your badge." She does. "Wait here."

I slip down the hallway to the room that matches the number of the key—302. I tap her badge to the reader and step inside, closing the door behind me. I see the desk with a picture of her and Emily on it, and I take the computer from it. I grab a duffel bag from under the bed, opening the dresser and emptying a few drawers into it. When I see her underwear, I freeze. I close my eyes as I palm a handful of them, throwing them into the bag. Then I zip it up and walk back out of the door. I take her hand as I walk by, leading her down the stairs. Then we hurriedly get into the back of the car where Russ is waiting.

"To the apartment, please, Russ," I say, handing her her things. She looks at me. "One step at a time."

She's silent on the ride, staring out over the lights as we finally pull back into Manhattan. She goes to grab her bag as Russ parks in the garage, but I yank it up from the seat before she can grab it. Russ opens her door and helps her out, and then we're on the elevator back up to my apartment. Where she can breathe. Where I can keep an eye on her.

Where she feels like mine.

Fuck. Why am I letting this happen?

I know this is all just stemming from the trauma of the last week, but I can't ignore the pull I feel toward her, thinking about how alone she must feel with no family on this side of the country. Her closest friend here was gunned down by a maniac. She had to watch students like herself get blown to shit while she was just trying to get back to her goddamn dorm room.

I'm infuriated all over again just thinking about it. But I don't have time to dwell on it right now. She needs me.

As we make our way into the apartment, I let Russ know he can lock up and head out. The night guard will switch out with him and post up outside the door. My security team is not one to reckon with, and I'm thankful for them every single day.

Emily has shut down the kitchen, and the penthouse is quiet. I set her bag down on the island and then lead her to the living room. She sits down on the couch, and I fight off a smile as she settles in, looking comfortable. Like she feels safe here.

I grab the remote and press a few buttons, and my eighty-inch television lowers down from the ceiling. I press another button, and the lights dim.

"How about something to drink?" I ask. She looks up at me and raises an eyebrow.

"Do you have beer?" she asks. I smirk.

"Yes, I have beer," I say, walking to the wine fridge and pulling out two bottles. I pop the tops then walk back to the living room, sitting down next to her. I grab the remote and put *Cheers* on, then I put my feet up on the coffee table.

"So," I say, casually taking a sip of my beer, "we gonna talk about it, or are we just gonna watch?"

I see her take a sip of hers out of the corner of my

eye, but I don't take my eyes off the screen. She fiddles with the bottle, then she sighs.

"I know," she says. "I'm fucked up."

"What?" I ask. She stares down at the top of her bottle.

"This whole thing...I just don't know how to get over it. I don't feel normal. I feel like I'm just going through the motions."

I think for a minute.

"Sawyer, I don't know that this is something you ever get over. This is...this is big. This is something no one should ever have to go through. This is severe trauma."

She shakes her head, drawing in a deep breath and pulling her legs into her body.

"No, that's just it, though," she says. "I didn't go through it the way other people did. My friends who were locked away or who freakin' died. I got away. I got saved. I got off easy."

I see her lip trembling, and she bites it. I reach over and take her hand.

"Sawyer, just because you didn't have more damage done doesn't mean there was none. Thank God you didn't. But just because others did, that doesn't mean that you deserved it. You still saw him. You watched people die. Sawyer, that's not normal. You're not supposed to just get over something like that." She nods after a moment. "Have you...have you thought about talking to someone?"

She shrugs.

"Carrington is offering free counseling to every student. But...I don't know. I just feel like they have people to help who need it more than I do."

God, this girl. She doesn't even feel like she deserves help.

"I see," I say. "Well, if and when you feel ready, I have a therapist that I've worked with for years. He has his own practice, and there is a new female therapist who specializes in trauma. If I give you their information, promise you'll think about it?"

She shakes her head.

"I can't afford that," she says. And before I can say anything, she sticks a finger in my face. "And no, you may not pay for it."

I laugh.

"Wasn't going to pay for it," I say. "I actually am an investor in the practice, so I get free services. It would be free for you."

She thinks for a minute, biting her lip again.

"Okay," she says. "I'll think about it."

I smile.

"Good."

"I'm really sorry I called you," she says, and I almost choke. I swallow and put my drink down on the table, looking at her.

"What?" I say.

"I thought I'd be able to handle it," she says, swirling her thumb around the top of her bottle. "But when I got to that door, I just...couldn't. And I just..." Her voice trails off as she laughs to herself, rubbing her temple. "I couldn't call my mom because it would destroy her if she knew I needed her, and she couldn't get to me. And all my friends are dealing with the same shit, or are still with their families, or are dead... How sad is it that the only person I could call was the billionaire I met a few weeks ago who was nice enough to clothe and house me?"

I know how she means it. I know that, much like everyone else in my life, she assumes that I hold myself to a higher standard, that my busy is more important than everyone else's busy, that I couldn't possibly be bothered by the problems of the rest of the world.

And until about a week ago, some of that might have been true.

But considering the fact that I've had more intimate moments with her in the last week that I've known her than with any other woman I've been with over the last decade, I thought we might be past that.

"Ouch," I say with a half-smile, picking my beer back up and looking back at the TV.

"I'm sorry...I...I just..."

I put the bottle back down and turn myself toward her.

"You better call me every fucking time, Sawyer. Do you understand me?" I say, my voice firm. She swallows again, nodding slowly. I reach out and cover her hand with mine. "Do you know how I got to campus so quickly tonight?" She shakes her head. "Because I came out there on purpose. Hoping you'd need me. Or at least hoping I could check in. Circling around like a damn vulture. So you better fucking call me. Every. Time."

She nods, her eyes big and wide, and I give her a half-smile again. And then I lean back on the couch and turn the volume up a few clicks.

An hour or two pass, and the number of empty bottles on the table in front of us has stacked up. Except that one of us is six-two, and the other is about five-three on a good day. So one of us is feeling it a little more than the other. And as we've sat, she's inched closer and closer to me, and I can't help but soak in the smell of her hair as she does. I try desperately to ignore the twitching in my pants as she curls in closer.

As we're finishing season three, she turns toward me, and now, it's not so subtle. And then, her head is resting on my shoulder. I clear my throat as I take a sip of the water I got myself when I got her last beer. I probably should have stopped her, but I figured she deserved a night to get shitfaced and not have to worry about anything. So I let her drink but slowed down myself so that I can be here if she needs me.

But as she nestles into me more, I realize that maybe she wants a little something extra. And it's much more than just a twitch in my pants now.

"Julian?" she asks.

"Hmm?"

"Why were you waiting outside of campus? Why... why were you hoping I'd need you?" she asks, her big green eyes staring up at me. I reach my hand out and stroke her cheek gently with my thumb.

"Probably for the same reason you called me tonight," I whisper back. I push a stray piece of hair out of her face. She just stares at me, her eyes bouncing back and forth between mine. And then, before I can catch her, she pushes up on me, pressing her lips to mine in a sloppy, albeit delicious, kiss. I let it go on longer than I should, and before I know it, she's pushing up farther onto my lap, straddling me. I pull away from her as she's sliding her hands down my arms and toward my waistband.

"Sawyer, what are you doing?" I say as I look up at her. She tries to move her hands farther south, but I catch them in mine.

"You said yourself that you had to be close to me tonight," she breathes. "So just let it happen."

"Sawyer..." I say, and she keeps wriggling, slowly moving her hips back and forth on mine. I pin both of her wrists in one hand and use my other to steady her hips.

"Julian..."

I chuckle while I hold tight to her hands and hips as she struggles to break free of my grasp. "This is what we call a trauma bond, sweetheart. You're drunk, and I'm not fucking you tonight."

She stops moving, her eyes big and wide. I lean forward, pulling her face to mine and leaving one last light kiss on her lips.

"Lie down," I whisper against her lips. She looks at

me, confused. I hook a hand under one of her knees and flip her onto the couch. I grab one of the pillows and put it in my lap, then I pat it. She just stares at me.

My god, I can't believe I have this much restraint.

Slowly, she crawls closer, putting her head down on the pillow in defeat. I turn the volume on the TV down a little, and then I stroke her hair slowly while the next season starts. Within moments, she's out, snoring gently on my lap.

I could get used to this.

Fuck. No.

She is a *student*. She's just been through some traumatic, once-in-a-lifetime shit—well, hopefully.

And I come with my own baggage.

I should really leave her be.

But having her here, safe in my home and in my care?

It just feels really fucking good.

SAWYER

I feel the sun streaming in on my face, and I open my eyes slowly. I realize I'm not on the couch, and I sit up. My hangover headache sets in, and I rub my temples, thinking back to last night. I vaguely remember him waking me up at some point, telling me to go up to bed. Then I remember him carrying me up his stairs and bringing me to the guest room I stayed in last week.

I could get used to sleeping in this massive bed.

No, I couldn't.

I shake my head as I get out of bed, walking toward the bathroom. And then I freeze in

my tracks when I remember what else I did last night. I smack my forehead with my hand as I cringe, thinking of how I mounted him and tried to seduce him in my drunken splendor.

"Oh, my god," I whisper to myself as I let my hands slide down my face.

I *never* do stuff like that.

Trevor Bell was my first and only boyfriend, and it took over a year for us to go out on our first date because I was too nervous to say yes. I have had a couple of random hookups over the last three and a half years, but they've all left me wondering what the fuck everyone freaks out about sex for.

But there is something about Julian that makes my entire body ache in the best way. It feels like parts of me are awake now that have been dormant my entire life. And I really like it.

But I can't like it enough to make a complete fool of myself when he was kind enough to take me in... again.

I splash water on my face, comb my fingers through my hair, then take the walk of shame—the not-so-fun kind—down the massive staircase to the living room. When I round the corner into the kitchen, though, I'm surprised to see a platter full of food and Russ at the kitchen island, sipping coffee and watching the morning news.

"Morning," he says when he sees me.

"Morning," I say, looking around.

"He left," Russ says. "Said to tell you he was sorry he had to run. He has a meeting-packed day today, but I'll give you a ride."

I nod, trying to cover my disappointment.

Oh, God. I definitely gave him the ick last night. He's having his people handle me.

Fuck.

"Bonnie made you a few different things," he goes on. "Eat something before we leave." I nod again, walking slowly toward the platter of hot foods she made and stabbing at a pancake and a few pieces of bacon before I take a seat next to him at the island. I grab the syrup, and Russ and I watch the weather report in silence for the next fifteen minutes. I finish up and bring my plate to the sink.

"Just leave it," he says.

"I don't mind washing it," I tell him. He smirks.

"Honey, the people that work in this kitchen get paid a lot more than I do. Leave it," he says, standing up. Russ is a tall Black man with both bulging biceps and a bit of a gut, but he still looks like a dude I wouldn't want to fuck with. Or maybe like a dude I'd want with me if someone *else* was trying to fuck with me.

"You ready?" he asks as I throw away my napkin. I nod. My bag is packed and on the floor where I left it last night, and Russ bends down to grab it.

"I already have the other things we brought back in the car downstairs," he says.

"Thank you," I say, trying not to take it personally that it feels like he's trying to get me out of here fairly quickly. I wonder what his instructions were.

"Feed her, then get her out of my apartment." Maybe something to that effect.

We take the elevator down, and he helps me into the back of the Escalade, then he puts my bag inside the other door. He pulls out, and I take a mental picture of everything as we leave, knowing I'll likely never set foot in a billionaire's apartment ever again. I sigh as I stare out the window, visibly pouting.

Not only will I miss the amenities and the incredibly sexy billionaire who owns them, but this means I have to go back to campus. For the first time since my entire world got upended, I have to face it. Alone.

But as we get off on the exit toward campus, I notice he doesn't take our usual route. And then he keeps veering off, about two miles east, closer to the water.

"Where are we going, Russ?" I ask. But he doesn't answer. Instead, he pulls the car onto a side street, right on the beach. He parks in front of a set of row homes, and then he gets out. He opens the back door and grabs my bags then walks around to let me out. He leads me up one of the stoops, enters a code, then pulls the door open when it unlatches.

Then I follow him up a set of stairs and then one more. We pass several doors, and I realize the row homes have been converted to apartments. And when we get to the next floor, he walks me to a door then hands me a single silver key.

I take it, looking up at him, confused as hell.

He nods toward the door, and I unlock it.

When it opens, my jaw drops.

It's the cutest, most perfect little apartment. There's a kitchen when we first walk in, a living room with a small couch and TV in front of us, and a single door to the right. I turn back to him.

"Where are we?"

He sets my bags down on the floor then nods toward the door. I walk to it and open it, and inside is the coziest little bedroom I've ever seen. A queen bed sits in one corner, a small desk in the other. And at the back of the room is a large round window with a perfect view of the ocean.

"Oh, my god," I whisper, taking it all in. Russ clears his throat, and I look at him. He nods his head toward a piece of paper that's sitting on the bed.

I walk toward it and pick it up.

I hope this place gives your mind a little break for the rest of the school year. Look out at the water and breathe.

~J

P.S. Lease is signed for six months. No takebacks.

My jaw drops again, and I turn back to Russ who is standing with a big smile on his face. As we're standing there, his phone rings.

"Hey, boss," he says. "Yep, we're here now. Hold on one sec." He hands me the phone then walks out of the room.

"Julian," I start to say, but he cuts me off.

"Sorry I couldn't be there this morning," he says. "I am running like a mad man today. I had one of my interior designers do some decorating, but there was only so much she could do with twelve hours' notice. We can get some more things if you want. Also, the couch has a pull-out mattress for when your mom comes to visit."

"Julian," I say, a lump forming in my throat, "you

can't...I can't do this. I can't let you *give* me an apartment."

He chuckles on the other end, and the sound of it makes my insides tingle.

"Sawyer," he says, and I relish the way my name sounds rolling off his tongue, "breathe. I have to hop into my next meeting. Go study in your new room."

Then the line goes dead. I walk out of the room and hand the phone back to Russ.

"Thank you," I tell him. He nods.

"The rest of your things have been moved out of your dorm. J got campus police to let us in last night. A few of his assistants unpacked last night, but apologies if things aren't where you want them. I just texted your phone a moment ago, so you have my number if you need it. Call us with any problems. J says he'll be checking in," Russ says, walking to the door.

"Thank you again, Russ," I say as he waves goodbye. I close and lock the door behind him, and then I turn back to my new home.

Breathe, he told me.

And that's exactly what I do as I walk toward my new couch, pull up my new throw blanket, and stare out at my new view.

SAWYER

I've been in my new apartment for two weeks, and every moment I spend in it, I feel myself feeling a little more normal again. I've been thinking more about the therapist that Julian referred me to, and it's starting to feel less scary. Now that I've had an escape, my brain feels less fogged. I feel like I'm ready to move on. To figure out how to move forward.

I pull out the card he gave me from my wallet and send off an introductory email to the practice. Here goes nothing.

Julian has checked in every day, but I've definitely been feeling the space between us, and I have to admit, that's had me more distracted than anything. Thanksgiving is next week, but I've decided not to go home. My mom is sad, and so am I, but I can't lose my job at the mini-mart. That's how I'll fund any expenses for my final semester here, groceries, parking passes, and anything else the college life wants to throw at me, and I can't afford to lose it now. So I'll stay, work as many shifts as I can, and save up to fly home for Christmas.

With campus closing next week and Julian being so busy, I'm bracing myself for the loneliness that I know is coming.

I'm lying on my couch, starting season four of *Cheers,* and scrolling on my phone when I get to an article about the shooting. I sit up as I read the head-line: *All victims' funerals paid for by anonymous donor.*

I take in a deep breath as I read about how not only were the funeral costs completely covered, but each family was also gifted two million dollars by the donor.

Oh, my god.

I click out of the article and open a text to him.

You're a good man, Julian Everett.

I wait a beat then see the dots appear on my screen.

He sends just a question mark, and I send the link to the article.

There's another pause, then he texts back.

I don't know what you're talking about, he says. *How's the apartment?*

I smile.

Amazing. I really can't thank you enough. Like I said, you're a good man, Julian.

He ignores my compliments.

What are you doing?
Starting season four.
Without me?

I smile and bite my lip.

You're welcome to step away from boring billionaire grown-up life and join.

I press send, and then I immediately feel my stomach turn. I think I just tried to proposition Julian Everett. Again.

I see the read receipt pop up. My stomach flips again. I see dots then nothing.

I wait a few minutes.

Still nothing.

Fuck. I just propositioned Julian Everett, and he rejected me. Again.

I lie back on the couch and turn the TV up, trying to drown out the voice in my head that's reminding me how fucking embarrassing I am. I stare at the television, letting my foot bounce on the ground for an entire episode. I check my phone one last time then throw it down on the coffee table. I lie back on the couch then grab one of my throw pillows and hold it against my face, letting out a frustrated scream into it.

As I'm in the midst of my theatrics, I jump at a loud knock on my door. I swallow as I slink off the couch, tiptoeing across my own living room to look through the peephole.

Oh, my god.

I run a hand through my hair and then swallow as I unlock the door and open it.

"Hi," I say. His hair is perfectly combed and styled, and he's got a suit on that sends that white-hot heat between my legs.

"Hi," he says. "Get dressed. We're going out."

JULIAN

J'm sitting on the living room couch in her apartment—which is technically *my* apartment—while she gets ready, and I am realizing how fucking stupid I am. I was practically giddy when she texted me earlier, and when she not-so-subtly asked me to join her, I turned into a horny teenage boy. It wasn't till I was halfway here that I realized I can't fuck her.

It wouldn't be right.

She's attached to me. The whole *hero syndrome* thing.

She's completely vulnerable, and I won't do it to her. I can't give her what she needs.

So instead, I'm taking her to dinner, and I'll slowly torture myself all fucking night.

And when she walks out of her room in a long black dress that ties around her neck, I want to kick myself. How the fuck am I supposed to focus on *not* fucking her when she looks like *this*?

"Wow," I say as I stand up. She swallows as she looks up at me.

"Is this okay? I don't really have anything else nice." I take a step closer to her, breathing her in and eyeing her from head to toe.

"It's perfect," I say, holding my hand out toward the door.

Tyler drives us about a half-hour outside of town to a favorite restaurant of mine, this little spot with a lot of private booths. We called ahead, so they take us to our table as soon as we get there, and we go unnoticed.

I order a bottle of wine for the table and a few appetizers. She picks at them while she looks at the menu.

"Sixty bucks for one steak? Jesus," she says under her breath, and I laugh.

"You're not paying, so it doesn't matter," I say. I see her go to open her mouth, and I stop her. "Sawyer, Everett Enterprises brings in over four hundred thousand dollars every single minute. Do me a favor. When you're with me, let yourself forget about money. Deal?"

Her eyes are as big as saucers, and she swallows. She bites her bottom lip then clears her throat.

"In that case," she says, "I'll get the lobster." She smiles, and I laugh again. God, I want her. After we put our orders in, she turns her body toward me and takes another sip of her wine.

"Okay," she says. "Tell me what growing up Everett was like."

I smile as I take another sip myself.

"You said you did the research," I say. I hate talking about my family. One, because there are already so many narratives that have been floating around for over a century about us. Two, because I'm not particularly proud of some of my family's history—or present, for that matter.

"I did," she says. "But I'm asking you. Tell me what it was like."

I sigh as I look at her. I know she's not going to let this go, and for some reason, I don't feel as uncomfortable as normal about sharing it.

"It was a dream in a lot of ways. Palatial homes in ten different countries, celebrity parties, all the things you can imagine are true. But it all comes at a cost. You don't get to be king of the world without losing some things."

She looks back at me intently.

"What did you lose?" she asks.

"The right to anonymity, for one thing," I chuckle. She gives me a pity smile, but I know she's waiting for more. "Nothing is sacred, nothing is private. The money always comes first. And you learn quickly that if it came down to the money or you, your parents would choose the money. Money over everything."

Her eyebrows knit together as she studies me, and

suddenly, I'm aware that I just shared more with her than I have with anyone else. And it's a foreign feeling.

Just as I'm about to change the subject, I see two people approaching our table out of the corner of my eye.

Fuck.

"Julian," the woman says. I clear my throat as I stand up. I was really hoping I would never run into her again...or her husband.

"Ana," I say as we stand awkwardly for a moment before she goes in for the double cheek kiss. Doug appears from behind her, awkwardly sticking out a hand for me to shake. "How have you all been?"

Ana looks at me, then to Sawyer, then back to me, an eyebrow raised.

"We've been well," Doug says sheepishly from behind her. I nod.

"We were expecting, uh...to hear from you," Ana says, her eyes trailing back to Sawyer. "But it appears you've been busy." She laughs nervously, but I don't. I scoot slightly closer to Sawyer, as if that could protect her from this.

"Busy, indeed," I say, giving her a look. She signed an NDA, and this conversation is technically going against it. When she senses that the air is a little less friendly, she clears her throat and smiles again.

"Right, well, I'll let you get back to your evening," she says. "Let's go, Doug. It was great to see you again, Julian."

"Have a good evening," I say as they walk by us, and I take my seat again.

Sawyer's eyes are big again, and she's staring at me with a mixed look of confusion and intrigue.

"What was *that?*" she asks, and I chuckle at how she can't help herself.

I should lie.

I should make something up.

I shouldn't show her this side of me.

But then something tells me that, with her, it's better to get it all out in the open. I'm not particularly proud of the different lifestyles I've tried on in my life, but I've had enough therapy to understand why I've tried them. I'm not mad at myself. And there are some reasons that I still stand by.

"We used to, uh..." I say, waving a finger between myself and the direction that Ana and Doug walked off in.

Her eyes stay wide.

"And her husband knows?" she asks. I clear my throat as I take another sip of my wine, then I look back at her. A little gasp leaves her lips. "Oh, my...was he...he was...he was *there?*"

JULIAN

I don't say anything, I just lean back against the booth and watch as she works through this new information.

"Is that...is that something you've done with... multiple, uh, partners?" she asks nervously. I narrow my eyes at her.

Time to rip off the Band-Aid.

"It is."

She swallows again.

"I'm sorry, I...I just want to make sure I'm understanding. Are you...are you saying that you fuck women in front of their husbands?" she asks.

"I'm saying that I have."

Her eyes move a thousand miles a minute back and forth as she processes. I laugh as I take another sip of my wine.

"Tell me," I say after a few moments, "who are you judging more: me or them?"

Finally, she raises her eyes to me.

"I'm trying not to judge anyone," she says. "I just have so many questions." I smile.

"Ask away."

"How...how do you know when they...when someone might be into it?"

"The people who are into it normally have a tell."

"What kind of tell?" she asks.

I smirk again as I take one more swig of my wine.

"They ask a lot of questions."

I watch as the pink flushes her cheeks, and she tucks a piece of hair behind her ear. She squirms in her seat, and I lean forward across the table.

"Ask me what you want to ask me," I say. She raises her eyes to me again.

"Does that...is that satisfying for you?" she asks. I pause for a moment. I've never really put that much thought into it. It's not something I've done a lot, only a few couples throughout my adult life.

"It's not so much about the satisfaction," I say, "but more about the lack of attachment."

Her eyebrows knit together. "Remember what I just told you? Money over everything. For most of the world, I'm a walking, talking dollar sign. I don't do relationships because there isn't a great track record of women who are interested in me more than they are my last name or my net worth. Ana, Doug, people like that, make it a little bit easier to walk away because we all know going in that it will never be anything more. I don't trust anyone. Sex is easier. I don't know who any of them are. Half the time, I don't even know their names, whether their husbands are with us or not. Usually, it's a one-and-done situation."

She narrows her eyes at me then nods slowly.

"That makes sense, actually," she says, and I am taken aback. I lean back in the booth again, putting one arm up on the top of the seat. I smile at her.

"Does it?" I ask. She nods as she finishes her glass.

"Yeah," she says. "You've never known uncondi-tional love, so you don't trust people. It's easier for you to connect, physically only, to people who are also off-limits."

I look her up and down, and I cannot fight this stupid smirk on my face.

I just told this girl about my slutty past, and she barely batted an eye.

"You are somethin' else, Sawyer," I say.

The ride home is quiet, and as she looks out the window, I feel myself growing uneasy. Is she rethinking what she's learned about me? Maybe it's for the best. Help break the attachment now rather than later down the road.

But the thought of her not calling, not needing me, not wanting me around, makes me more anxious than I care to admit.

When we get back to the building, I walk her up to the apartment. She unlocks the door, and as I'm about to say goodnight, she grabs my arm.

"I know you know my name," she says, "but if you

ever decide that's not a deal-breaker, just know that I'm pretty good at keeping my mouth shut."

Holy fuck.

If she only knew...

I take a step closer to her so she's backed up against the door. I reach my hand up and stroke her cheek gently, then I lean down and press my lips to her jawline, then again to her neck. I feel my dick as hard as a fucking brick in my pants, and it's taking all my restraint not to tear this fucking dress off her right now.

"I told you, sweetheart, I'm not fucking you," I whisper in her ear. "And believe me, it's not because I don't want to. But if I did, there would be plenty for that pretty mouth of yours to do besides stay shut."

I leave one more kiss on her shoulder, then I push her door open and nudge her gently inside before closing it and walking back down to the car with the biggest hard-on I've ever fucking had.

SAWYER

$\mathcal{I}$ stand against the wall to the entryway of my apartment for a few minutes, trying to replay everything that just happened. For the second time now, I've been rejected by Julian Everett. But he does it in a way that somehow still lets me know that he wants me in some capacity. It's confusing as hell.

I'm not fucking you. And believe me, it's not because I don't want to.

What the fuck does that even mean? Is it because I'm too young? Too...vulnerable? Too...what? Available?

I run a hand down my face and force myself to take a cold shower before my brain creates every possible scenario and reason for him not taking me up on my offer.

* * *

THE NEXT MORNING, I'm up early for my shift at the mini-mart. I have a beat-up bike that I occasionally use to get around campus, but the cold air is welcome this morning after a long night of burning loins.

I've checked my phone approximately twenty-seven times since he dropped me off about eight hours ago, but I have yet to see his name light up my phone. And after rejection number two, the little bit of pride I have left is all that's keeping me from texting him first. I round the last corner to the shop but stop dead in my tracks when I see the black Escalade parked right out front. I tuck a piece of hair behind my ear and keep walking, clearing my throat as I get closer to the car. The door opens, and I hold my breath but quickly blow it out when I see Tyler walking toward me.

"Morning, Sawyer," he says with a tip of an imaginary hat.

"Morning," I say with one eyebrow raised. He lifts something from behind his back, and I want to kick myself when I realize it's my purse.

"Left this in the car last night," he says. "Boss wanted me to get it to you."

I smile faintly as I take it.

"Oh, Jesus," I say, "thanks for bringing it back."

Not only did I leave it in his car, but I wouldn't have even realized it until Tyler showed up.

He must sense me looking past him, because he smiles faintly.

"Boss has lots of meetings today, but he wanted me to tell you to give me a ring if you need anything."

I screw my face up.

"I'm fine, but thank you, Tyler. And if I don't see you before, have a great Thanksgiving," I tell him. He nods as I turn on my heel and walk into the store.

I put my stuff on the shelf under the counter, clip my name tag on, and log into the register computer.

The normal coffee grabbers will be in within the next few minutes, but I have some time to stew. Not only did he send Tyler to deliver my purse for me—which, I guess, I should be much more appreciative of—but then he also sent a message. One that felt like, "*Hey, don't bug me. Use my hired help instead.*"

Ick.

I know one thing is for certain: having my sexual advances rejected and then getting pushed off on his errand boy within a twenty-four-hour timespan doesn't feel awesome.

Maybe he really does want me; maybe that was bullshit. But either way, he's not getting shit. I work my shift, close up shop, and go home, and the only person I've texted all day is my mom. As I'm walking back down the street, I dial her.

"Hi, baby," she says. "How was your shift?"

"It was fine," I say. "It's freezing now, though."

"It sure is. It's cold here too. How's the new place? I still can't believe he did that. I just can't believe it. I texted him to—"

"You texted him?" I ask, cutting her off.

"Yes, is that a problem? He gave my child a home. I

thought it might be rude for me not to at least thank him."

God dammit.

"He gave me his number before I flew back home. An incredible man, honestly. I know what people think about his family, and maybe it's true, but him...wow."

"He gave you his number?" I ask.

"Yes. He told me to feel free to check in, or if I ever had any problems getting a hold of you, or anything, to call him. He wanted me to know that someone was there for you on that side of the country."

Stupid dick.

Stupid, sweet, compassionate dick.

"Is there a problem, Sawyer?" she asks. "Did something happen? I'll cut him. What happened?"

I almost laugh at how quick she flips her switch when it involves me.

"No, Mom," I say. "Nothing happened. I just didn't know, that's all."

"Ah, okay," she says. "Are you back to your apartment?"

"Walking up the steps right now," I say, plugging the code into the front door.

"Good," she says. "I still can't believe it. I can't wait to see it. I'm sad we won't be together for Thanksgiving."

"I know, Ma," I say, holding the phone between my ear and my shoulder to unlock my door. "Me too. But I need to get a few more shifts in before the holidays.

And I don't want Jake to think I'm not coming back and fire me. I need this job."

She sighs on the other end.

"I know, honey. I know. I just miss you, that's all."

"I miss you too, Mom," I say. "I love you."

"I love you, baby. Call me tomorrow."

"I will. Bye," I say, hanging up.

I turn on my shower after I throw my things down on the table and walk back into my bedroom. I peel off my clothes and head for the bathroom just as my phone dings on my bed. I freeze when I see his name.

I pick it up embarrassingly fast and slide it open.

Are you off yet?

I scoff. Why does he care? I debate not answering at all. I really shouldn't. I should end this weird little thing we have. So, being the strong-willed woman I am, I wait all of thirty seconds to respond to him.

Just got home. I pause for a moment, biting my lip before adding, *About to get in the shower.*

I wait for a response, but nothing. I wait another twenty seconds. Nothing.

Fuck. I shouldn't have answered. I throw my phone back on my bed and get in the shower.

I try to relax, take my time, wash the day off of me, but my body is racing through the motions of washing itself. My brain is saying, *Who gives a shit? Let him wait.* While my heart—and my vagina—are telling me to get back to that phone as fast as humanly possible.

I turn the water off, wrap a towel around me, and practically run out to my bedroom.

What are you doing tomorrow?

I swallow. Tomorrow is Thanksgiving. Why is he asking? There is no way Julian Everett doesn't have plans for Thanksgiving. I think about making something up so I don't sound so pathetic. But then I remember he's seen me at the most vulnerable I've ever been in my life. There's really no use in hiding.

Sitting in my robe with a book. Why do you ask?

I'd like to take you somewhere. Pick you up at ten?

My heart rate starts to pick up. I really shouldn't let him affect me like this.

Where?

Think of it as a little Thanksgiving surprise. Ten?

I sigh as I stare down at my phone, biting my lip. I tap my foot on the ground for a moment.

Fine. Ten.

That man is so confusing. So frustrating.

And so fucking delicious. And coincidentally, I'm already naked. So I hop into my browser, image search him, and lie back on my bed like I have *way* too many times since I met him.

SAWYER

I'm up early as usual, lying in my bed and staring out at what has become my favorite view. I love the gray-blue color of the early morning sky over the black water before the sun blazes through any of it. It feels like, when I get up this early, I'm the only one who gets to see it in this state. Untouched but still beautiful in its own right without the glow of the sun.

I make myself some breakfast, putz around the apartment, then start to frantically get myself ready as time ticks closer to ten. As I'm sifting through my closet, though, I realize I don't know how to dress. I grab my phone and dial him, not bothering to send a text first.

"Are you bailing on me?" he asks, and I can hear the smirk in his voice. I bite my lip to keep from smiling back.

"You never told me what to wear," I say, ignoring him.

"Hmm," he says. "How about you wear what you were wearing last night when we were texting?"

I think for a minute, confused.

"But I wasn't—oh," I say. He chuckles on the other end of the line as that same white-hot heat rushes between my legs.

"Wear whatever you want. It's just you and me," he says. "See you soon."

Fuckkkk. Why does he do this?

And why does my body react this way?

As much as I probably should have said no to this excursion, I also am telling myself that I need to be with him again to get a temperature on things. If he was serious about never fucking me, then I need to take this "relationship" for what it is: a much older man who happens to be in the top one percent of the entire fucking world, who saved me from a mass shooting and occasionally checks in with my mom. Totally normal.

I decide on an old Carrington hoodie, my old Nikes, and a pair of jeans. And before I know it, there's a knock on my door. I take a breath as I grab my bag and walk to the door. When I open it, the breath rushes from my lungs at the sight of him, his dark hair waving just right, his ripped arm muscles bulging out of the long-sleeved tee he has on. He doesn't look like a billionaire. He looks like...I don't know...someone I want to fuck.

Fuck.

"Morning, sunshine," he says with a killer smile. I flash a quick one back and brush by him.

"Morning," I say, slamming the door shut behind him.

"Whoa," he says with a little giggle, but when I don't turn around, he snags my arm. "What's going on?"

I sigh. He called me. He arranged this. He's taking me somewhere, and he gave me a fucking *home.* I force a smile.

"Nothing," I say. "Just...missing my mom. Sorry." He smiles and pulls me in for a hug. Then he takes my hand and leads me down the stairs and to the Escalade. Russ lets us in, then we're off.

"So, are you gonna tell me yet?" I ask as we pull out of my neighborhood.

He smiles.

"Mighty impatient, aren't we?" he asks. I smile and shrug. *You have no idea.* "Have you ever heard of Bedell House?"

I look up at him.

"Like the mansion?" I ask. He smirks. "Oh, yeah! I totally forgot you guys owned that. Is that where we're going?"

He nods.

"They start putting up all the Christmas decorations today before they open to the public for holiday tours tomorrow. I thought you'd like a sneak peek. And maybe a personal tour."

I smile and nod.

"I'd love that," I say. "I've never been."

Thirty or so minutes later, we pull up to a huge iron gate with a screen and buttons. Russ types in a code then places his hand on some sort of scanner that then opens the gate. He drives through, and I see nothing but sprawling, grassy hills and the tree-lined driveway in front of us.

As we get farther up the road, I see a huge parking lot on either side of the drive and signs that read *Public and Tour Parking*. Then farther up, we come to the crest of a hill, and you can see everything: the whole manor, the rocks, the ocean, the private beaches.

My jaw drops as Russ pulls us farther down the drive to the huge circle at the front. As he opens my door, I'm still in awe, staring up at the old-school architecture.

Let's call Bedell House what it is: a palace. It has wing after wing, story after story of brick and stone with ivy climbing up its walls as if to lead my eyes where to look next. There are towers that perk up above the rest of the house with balconies that face the water and massive floor-to-ceiling windows that seem to cover the entire first level.

"Think my great-grandfather was overcompensating for something?" Julian says from next to me, snapping me out of my daydream. I laugh and shake my head.

"This is amazing," I say. He nods then takes a few steps up, reaching his hand out to me.

"Wait till you see the inside," he says, and I smile and take his hand. I follow him up the rest of the massive stone staircase, and huge doors open up as we approach them. I jump back, and he laughs.

"We had the sensors installed a few years ago," he says. We walk into the huge entryway, and I realize we're still holding hands. I am conscious of it, but I don't make a move to pull away, and I'm hoping he doesn't either. In the center of the foyer is what looks to be a thirty- or forty-foot Christmas tree. There are people all around it on ladders, decorating it.

There are also people in every corner of this level, setting up other decorations, lights, and gifts. A woman in heels, a tight pencil skirt, and an even tighter sweater walks through one of the doorways, carrying a clipboard and a radio. She's making commands through it, but when she sees us, she freezes.

"Julian!" she says, tucking the clipboard under her arm and click-clacking faster across the porcelain in our direction. She has long, curly blonde hair that hangs around her breasts, and I can smell her perfume from a mile away. She swiftly drapes her arms around his neck, holding him tight for an awkwardly long hug, and it's the first time he's let go of me since we stepped inside.

"Ella," he says, "how are you?"

They come apart, and I feel her eyes dart to me again and again as they catch up. I can't tell if she wants him to introduce us or if she wants him to pretend I don't exist.

"How are things coming?" he asks her.

"Great!" she says, holding her arms out. "We're ahead of schedule. Should be done in plenty of time for the holiday tours to start."

"Wonderful. Looking great as always," he says. She smiles as she looks back at me one more time.

"Is there anything I can do for you?" Ella asks, looking back to him.

"No, thanks," he says, reaching an arm back and wrapping it around me, scooting me up closer to him. Without any further explanation, we nod goodbye and walk through the main doorway.

I'm not sure how to feel about the interaction. It shouldn't be shocking that other women want him—he's an insanely gorgeous man who comes from American royalty.

But it doesn't mean I have to like it.

And I'm not sure how to feel about him not introducing me. Does that mean something? Nothing? Anything?

I shake it off as he leads me to a long hall.

"Aren't you supposed to be, like, telling me about the place?" I ask after a few more minutes of silence. I decide to stop myself from asking about Ella. He smiles.

"Sorry, I'm slacking," he says. "What do you want to know?"

I look up at him.

"Everything."

We turn down another corridor that's lined with massive windows that face a perfectly manicured courtyard.

"Well, my great-grandfather started construction on this place in 1886, after the oil boom. It took twenty-six years to actually finish the first phase. The west wing wasn't added until my grandfather had it built after World War II," he says. We walk farther, and I feel him get closer to me, his hand brushing against my back as he leads me farther down. "These rooms here were originally guest suites for diplomats, business partners, other rich assholes my great-grandfather was trying to impress. They were later converted into event rooms for weddings and mitzvahs, things like that."

I smile as I watch him. I stop moving and tug at his hand.

"This is all really cool," I say, "but tell me the things I can't find on Google." He raises an eyebrow at me. "Give me *your* tour, Julian."

The corners of his lips turn up as he narrows his brown eyes at me. Then he nods and reaches for my hand again.

"Alright," he says, "this way." He leads me to the end of the hallway and opens up a huge door that spills us out into some other corridor. We walk a few yards down before a staircase appears to our left. It's chained off with a sign that reads, *No visitors beyond this point.* He steps over it and holds his hand out for me to do the same.

We walk up the huge staircase and to another set of huge doors. There's another one of those keypad things, and he types in a code and puts his hand on it like Russ did outside. It scans his palm then unlocks, and he opens it.

"You won't find this on Google," he says with a smile.

"Where are we?" I ask him.

"This is the east wing," he says. "After we opened the house to the public in the seventies, my grandfather kept this portion untouched. It was reserved for the family. It has a private entrance from outside, so we could come and go as we pleased without interrupting the tours or being seen by anyone. Now, hardly anyone uses it—just my brothers and I occasionally." We walk through another long corridor that opens up to a huge sitting room with a large stone fireplace and four big couches. There's a huge wooden dining room table at the far end of the room, which must have at least thirty chairs around it, with a massive antler chandelier hanging above it. "There's a full chef's kitchen back there, and then all of our suites are down this hall."

"You each have your own suite?" I ask. He nods.

"My parents, my aunt and uncle, and then each of us six grandkids had our own: me, my two brothers, and our three cousins. Then on the other side"—he points down the other end of the hall—"are five guest suites. We'd do every holiday here when we were kids."

"I bet that was like magic," I say, spinning around as I take everything in. I want to keep my composure, but this is really fucking cool. "Where's your suite?"

He looks up at me, raising an eyebrow again. He draws in a sharp breath then pushes off the couch and walks past me, leading me down to the third door on the wall. He turns the knob, and we walk down another shorter hallway that leads to *another* door. He opens that one, and we walk into a sitting room that leads into a huge bedroom. A king-sized four-post bed sits against the far wall, the big windows on the other, facing the ocean, and huge French doors that lead out to a balcony sit at the back corner of the wall. There's another fireplace in here, another couch, and an open doorway to a huge bathroom.

"Damn," I say, walking toward the bed. I drag my fingers across the comforter slowly, staring down at it. "I bet it didn't hurt to have this place to bring women back to."

I don't know why I say it, and I immediately regret it when I do.

I turn around to face him, and his eyes are narrowed on me again from across the room. Slowly, he paces toward me, and I swallow as he gets nearer and nearer.

89

"And what is it that you think I've done with these women here?" he asks, so close to me now that he has backed me up against the side of the bed. I swallow as I look up at him.

"Why don't you tell me?" I ask.

SAWYER

*H*e reaches a hand up to touch my cheek gently, his other hand snaking around my waist.

"Why don't you tell me, Sawyer? I want to know what you think I did. Did I touch them like this?" he asks, sliding his hand down the small of my back toward my ass, grazing it gently before he gives it a little squeeze. My breath catches in my throat. "Or like this?" he asks, sliding his other hand down my cheek and cupping the back of my neck.

Oh, fuck.

"Or did I kiss them like this?" he asks, and before I can say anything, his lips are on mine, hot and wet, hungry and impatient. I moan against his lips as both of his hands slide back to my ass, lifting me gently off the ground and laying me on the bed. I slide my hands up his arms and his back, letting my fingers get lost in that gorgeous head of hair of his. I feel myself getting

T.D. COLBERT

wet, and I wrap my legs around his waist, urging him to press himself into me.

Then I feel one of his hands slide around to my front, slipping between us, and my body starts to tingle. I press my body into the mattress further to give him easier access, just as his hand slides between my legs, over my jeans to my mound, where he rests it for a moment. But much to my dismay, he pulls apart from me, letting his forehead rest on mine for a second before he slides his hand out from between us.

No. No, no, no.

I lie still for a minute, waiting as he pulls himself off me and off the bed. I sit up, following him with my eyes as he takes a few steps toward the window, straightening himself out and looking out at the water.

This motherfucker. I am really sick of him giving me lady blue balls.

When it appears that our tryst—or lack thereof—is officially over, I speak.

"What do you want from me, Julian?" I ask. My stomach turns as I wait for his answer, but I need one. It's been three of the most intense weeks of my life, and I can't handle any more of this back and forth.

He sighs deeply before he turns to me.

"I don't know, Sawyer. But I know that I've never wanted it from anyone else."

I think about his response for a minute. It's incomplete, but it feels honest. And truth be told, I don't really know what I want from him either. A companion? A fuck buddy? All the above? Or maybe I just like him because of the clout? Maybe I just want to be near him because I associate him with safety?

I want to be mad. I want to throw a fit, but I can't. I don't have the right to. I wanted that just as much as he did. And I'm just as confused as he is.

I nod slowly as I slide off the bed.

We're quiet as he leads me back out of the family wing, down the private staircase, and into the elevator that takes us down to the private garage entrance. Russ picks us up there, and we're even more quiet on the way home. When we get back to the apartment, I feel this weird sense of melancholy.

I didn't get laid by my hot, pseudo-guardian, and now I have to eat a cup of noodles alone on Thanksgiving. When Russ pulls up to the building, I turn to Julian.

"You don't have to walk me up," I tell him. "I know you probably have very important Everett plans."

He glares at me for a moment then reaches down to undo his seatbelt as he gets out on his side. Russ helps me out, and Julian is on my side as he walks me up the front steps and enters the building code, completely ignoring me. We walk the three flights in silence, and just before we reach my door, he grabs my wrist, spinning me around to him.

"Don't you ever assume that any plans I ever have are more important than you. Ever," he says, staring down at me. I swallow as I look at him. Before I can respond, he reaches around me and opens my door, which I realize is unlocked. Before I turn around, he brings my hand to his lips.

"Happy Thanksgiving," he says with a smile. Then he pushes the door open wider, and my mother stands in my entryway, her pale-green apron tied around her waist, flour on her outstretched hands, and the smell of a turkey in the oven filling my apartment.

I gasp, tears filling my eyes as I run to her. She squeals as she catches me, spinning me around and kissing my head and cheeks. When we stop turning, she looks at him.

"Thank you, Julian," she says through tears. "You have no idea how much this means."

He smiles sheepishly, waving her off.

"I'm just glad you two get to be on the same coast for the holiday."

I stare at him in awe.

"You did this?" I ask.

"He's had it planned since you figured out you couldn't fly back, honey," she says. I feel a lump rise in my throat. She lets go of me, walking to him and throwing her arms around his neck. He hugs her back, looking at me. When he lets her go, I walk to him, following suit. I drape my arms around his neck, pressing up on my tiptoes so that my lips are next to his ear.

"Thank you, Julian," I whisper, and I feel his hold on me tighten.

He sets me down then clears his throat.

"Well," he says, "I'll let you ladies get to it."

"There is plenty of food if..." my mother starts to offer then probably realizes that she's offering the third richest man in the world to stay for dinner.

"I'd love to," he says, "but I want to let you two have some time together. And my father would kill me if I missed Thanksgiving." He smiles, backing up toward the door. "I'll check in tomorrow. , the jet is yours, so say the word, and we'll get it lined up when you need to get back."

She smiles and nods, putting her hands to her chest.

"Thank you, Julian," she says.

And as happy as I am to be with my mom right now, I'm equally as sad to watch him walk out of the apartment.

JULIAN

I would have literally given anything to stay in that apartment. Even if I couldn't have her to myself, just to be with her. Just to watch how happy she would be with her mom there. Just to see her laughing and smiling.

I'd give anything to be with her and *not* have to have Thanksgiving dinner with my own family. I take in a deep breath as Tyler peels away from the building, laying my head back against the leather headrest.

I close my eyes and replay the last few hours in my head, taking her to Bedell House, which, despite my complicated relationship with my family's legacy, is actually one of my favorite places in the world. It's one of the only places where I felt love. Where I saw it.

I loved watching her face as she took it all in, but mostly I loved when she asked about its secrets. She asks things that no one else would ever bother, or ever dare, to ask me.

And God, did I fucking *love* laying her down on that bed. Ravishing her lips. The things I wanted to do. The places I wanted to touch. The way I wanted to make her lose her pretty little mind.

And the fucking blue balls I got from stopping it all.

I'm in such a confusing place with her. I know our...friendship, for lack of a better word...is a bit unconventional and that it didn't begin in the healthiest of ways. I know I'm sending her all kinds of mixed signals, and I know it's not right, but I don't know what the fuck is going on. I tell myself I need to keep my distance—if for nothing else than to spare her any unwanted attention from the entire fucking world after an extremely traumatic event. But I also know that I need to keep my distance for *me*. Relationships are complicated when you come from a family like mine. I learned young that no one sees you for you. They see you for your family name, for fame, for old money. They see you for your rich father, your grandfather, your great-grandfather. They see you for the things they can acquire just by being near you.

They don't see you.

I've gotten close before. I've even put a ring on someone's finger. And then I found the full boxes of her birth control in my trash can. I found the internet searches on alimony and child support and trust funds before we were even fucking married.

And it broke my fucking heart.

I watched the way my parents tore each other

97

apart. I watched the way the world dragged my mother through the mud, because it must have been her. It couldn't have been my dad. Not Cato Everett. It must have been her doing nothing but gold digging. Not her giving him everything she could, including two sons, for him to schedule his island getaways with twenty-somethings while she was in the same room.

It couldn't be him.

I feel my blood pressure rise the closer we get to Bendmere, and to my father's estate out on the island. The home he had built when I was five, where I was raised. Not by my father, of course, but by my mother and by the people my father paid to raise me after he kicked her out.

Tyler enters the code, scans his palm, and pulls through and up the long driveway that looks like a shorter version of the one at Bedell House. The house is as big and obnoxiously grand as one would imagine, and he's had plenty of upgrades done to it as the years have passed. It sits at the farthest tip of the island, the only residence for three miles, as my father offered the state of Connecticut an obscene amount of money back in the eighties to purchase all the land in a four-mile radius for "privacy" reasons, which, in Cato language, just means he didn't want any peasants disrupting his views.

I hate this house.

Just as Tyler puts the Escalade in park at the front circle, I feel my phone vibrate in my pocket. I open it to a text from the one person I really needed a text from.

Thank you, Julian. I hope your Thanksgiving is as wonderful as you've made mine.

I look down at the phone with a dumb smile on my face, and suddenly, I feel like I can breathe again.

I hope you ladies eat all the turkey your hearts desire. Happy Thanksgiving, Sawyer.

I take a breath then slide out of the car. I thank the butlers for holding the door for me then the ones that take my coat. Angelina is the first to greet me, my father's third wife. She's two years older than me. Before they got married, my father got a vasectomy. He said three heirs was enough.

Heirs. Like it's a fucking kingdom.

Although, in some ways, it's even more than that.

It's a goddamn empire.

She runs to me, swallowing me in an overly enthusiastic hug, pressing her large breasts my dad bought her last year against me. I hug her back and hand her the bottle of champagne I brought her as a gift for hosting.

Behind her, I see my idiot brothers shooting me daggers, already with beers in their hand. I thank Angelina for having us then walk past her toward them.

Keaton is the middle brother. Typical middle-child syndrome, although none of us were ever hurting for much. He's three years my junior but, in some ways, feels so much younger than that. He's got a chip on his shoulder because he got even less time with our parents together than I did. He works out of the West

Coast offices in Santa Cruz and comes back as rarely as possible.

Brooks is the baby, known to the world as the bastard child. My father impregnated a nineteen-year-old masseuse while on a "work trip" when I was ten years old. Shortly after, he served my mom divorce papers, moved the woman from Italy to Bendmere, and married her. That marriage was even shorter than my parents', lasting just eleven months after Brooks was born. Brooks lives in the city too, but it's embarrassing how infrequently we see each other. My father has him paying his dues, working as a sales manager at one of our realty companies until he feels he's sweated enough. Not that it matters much, considering we were each handed four hundred million dollars when we graduated high school.

My father did everything he could not to give Brooks's mother, Marta, a single fucking dime. It wasn't until Brooks got his trust fund at eighteen that he could finally repay her for all she deserved.

Both of my brothers have a chip on their shoulder about Angelina. We've all seen this movie before. There was a contract signed along with the prenup. An undisclosed agreed-upon amount for if and when the marriage ends that she will walk away with. Not even a dent will be made in my father's fortune. And then the next year, the massive painted portrait above the grand fireplace will be replaced by his latest catch.

No use getting attached.

But me? They don't bother me anymore. Once I

saw what he was capable of doing to my own mother, whom I truly believed he loved at one point, I knew he could do it to anyone. I knew nothing was permanent. I'm jaded that way.

My mother died from breast cancer when I was twenty-one, right before I graduated from NYU. Otherwise, I'd be with her tonight and as far away from here as possible.

"Fucking Barbie," Brooks says as he throws back what's left in his bottle. I laugh as I pull him in for a hug.

"Easy there, big guy," I say, rubbing his head playfully, even though he's an inch taller than I am. He is the pretty brother, hands down. He's got his mom's Italian features: the tan skin, dark hair, full lips. But he has our father's eyes. He makes his looks work for him too. He's got quite the reputation as the playboy of the family. He's the one that used to be plastered all over the tabloids, drinking too much, partying on nude beaches in Spain or Italy.

"Brooksie just isn't used to a new mommy running around every week yet," Keaton says. He looks like our mother. Sandy-brown hair, gray eyes, tall and slender. I laugh as I pull him in for a hug too. Keaton is the intellectual of the three of us. He's the president of our media enterprises, but he's also been working to develop some sort of new concierge healthcare project. He knows we're richer than Midas. But like me, there's a part of him that knows how wrong it is that we have four houses in a thirty-mile radius, and millions of people have none.

Me, I'm the mule. The work horse of the family. The first born, sworn to fulfill the prophecy of running the world when it's my time. No time for my own ventures. I have Everett Enterprises to think about.

"How have you been, brother?" I ask, clapping Keaton's shoulder as Brooks hands me a beer. "How is the West Coast?"

"Still amazing," he says with a shrug. "You should really come out there more, if for nothing else than to get away from this fucking—hey, Pops!" he cuts himself off as Cato walks in the room. We all turn to him, and the air grows a little bit colder.

JULIAN

*C*ato is dressed in a perfectly tailored gray suit with no tie, shiny brown shoes—Givenchy, probably—with his hair slicked back in a perfect wave. He's got a little bit of stubble that gives him a bit of boyish charm, and he's still as fit as ever. My mom always said that if he never gave me anything else, at least he gave me good looks.

As much as I hate to admit it, I'm the spitting image of my dad.

He holds his hands out as Angelina appears at his side.

"My boys! God, I love it when you're all under one roof," he says, walking toward us with a big smile as she follows behind him like a puppy. He grabs Brooks first, kissing his cheek and hugging him.

"Hey, Dad," Brooks says. Then Keaton.

"Hey, Pops."

He pauses for a moment when he gets to me. He

waves his hand in my face playfully. "Eh, I see you all the time. But Happy Thanksgiving, Julian," he says as he pats my shoulder. I force a smile.

"Happy Thanksgiving, Cato."

I started calling him by his first name when I started working for the business. I couldn't walk into board meetings calling him "Dad." But then, it just sort of stuck. A few more of our relatives arrive: my dad's two sisters, their husbands and our cousins, and one of four great-aunts that's still alive.

We make painful small talk, pose for a few professional photos that will be slapped up on the family website, and then finally sit down to eat. My father's dining room has a table that's almost as grand as the one at Bedell House, seating thirty in a room with windows for walls that overlooks the sound. In the summer, the windows lift open, extending the room out onto the massive terrace.

My brothers and I all sit at one end of the table with a few more of our cousins, and once the food has been served, we all sort of break off into our own private conversations.

"So," Brooks says with a little devilish spark in his eye, "I called over to Bedell House this evening to see when the tours start. Talked to my boy Roadie."

I look up at him, eyebrows raised, as I take a sip of the shitty-tasting expensive wine that Angelina picked out. Fuckin' Roadie. He's one of the security managers on site at Bedell House. And he's got a big fuckin' mouth.

"Oh?" Keaton says, taking a bite of his food.

"Heard a certain brother of ours was on property today, with an unknown female guest. Saw them on the cameras entering the family quarters," Brooks says with a stupid smirk on his face as he takes a sip of his shitty wine. Keaton looks to him, then to me, then back to him.

"Julian?" he finally asks.

"Showing off the family digs now, are we?" Brooks says, playfully punching my shoulder.

"Fuck off, Brooks," I say, shaking my head as they both chuckle. *Fuck.*

"Who was she?" Keaton asks, dabbing his face with a napkin and looking up at me.

I shrug. No fucking way am I telling anyone—even my brothers—about her. The quieter I keep her, the more I can protect her.

"Don't worry about it," I say, punching Brooks back. "Asshole."

They both laugh again as my father clinks his glass and stands at the head of the table.

"Family, family," he says, "before we have the desserts brought out, I just wanted to take a moment to let you all know how grateful I am for each of you around this table. I am one of the luckiest bastards on this planet, and much of that is because of the family I surround myself with."

I almost snort in my wine.

Give me a fucking break.

"Happy Thanksgiving, everyone!" he says then sits back down.

I turn to my brothers again when I hear my father clear his throat.

"Oh, uh...did anyone see the news? An anonymous donor paid for all the funerals of the victims of the Carrington shooting."

My eyes dart to him, but he's already looking at me. There's a little bit of a pause.

"Well, that is certainly such a nice thing to do," my Aunt Madeline says. But my father never takes his eyes off me.

"Absolutely," he agrees. "Julian...didn't you give a speech at Carrington right around the same time as the shooting?"

I swallow the bite I've been chewing for too long and look at him.

"I was supposed to. It got postponed, for obvious reasons," I say. I know what he's trying to do. To the ignorant eye, it may look like a father who's proud of their child's selflessness, charity, philanthropy.

But to me, the trained eye of the son of Cato, I know he's trying to take the anonymity out of it. He wants the Everett name attached to it. He wants the credit.

Which is precisely why I paid for everything out of my personal accounts rather than any account attached to any of the businesses, so he had no line of sight to it.

He nods slowly, realizing he's not going to win this

one. There won't be any big admission tonight that he can slip to one of his PR managers tomorrow.

We glare at each other in a standoff for what feels like forever, until the servers come out to take our plates and bring dessert.

"It was you, wasn't it?" Brooks says to me once the room has filled with chatter again. "Carrington, the funerals. It was you."

I take a bite of my cheesecake.

"I don't know what you're talking about," I say.

"Come on, Julian," he pushes.

"Let it go, Brooks," Keaton chimes in, glaring at him. Brooks clears his throat and leans back. Keaton gets it. Brooks...he's not there yet. He's the baby. My dad was in his late forties when Brooks was born. He was spoiled—even more than Keaton and I had been —and coddled in so many ways. It wasn't until these last few years that Cato realized the monster he had created and began teaching Brooks some life lessons on hard work.

Finally, when the dessert plates have been collected, my brothers and I give each other *the look* as we all text our drivers. The appropriate amount of time has come, and we can leave without it looking like we dined and dashed.

"Who's gonna go first?" Keaton asks.

"Me!" Brooks says, almost shouting. "You guys got to bail first on Easter."

I laugh and shake my head. Another reason to never marry or have kids. May I never have the type of family where my kids fight over who gets to leave me first.

"Go ahead, Brooks," I say. He hugs us both then makes his way to the grand sitting area to say his goodbyes.

"How long are you in town?" I ask Keaton as we both check the time over and over until it's been an appropriate break between us and Brooks.

"I was going to fly back tomorrow," he says.

"Do you have time for breakfast in the morning?" I ask. He nods.

"That would be awesome," he says with a smile. He looks down at his watch. "Ready?" I nod.

We find Dad and Angelina, say our painful good-byes, and bolt for the door.

"I'll text you tomorrow?" I call out to Keaton as he gets in the car that pulls up for him.

"Sounds good!" he calls back.

I get in the car and tell Tyler to take me back to my apartment. I blow out the breath I've been holding all night as I look down at my phone, opening the text she sent me earlier.

I hope your Thanksgiving is as wonderful as you've made mine.

Little does she know that it was. And it was all because of her.

JULIAN

I wake up the next morning, staring out at the city from my bed. I need to get up and go workout, but all I can think about is her.

Before I know it, my hand wraps around my cock, hard as a brick with just the thought of her. Those dark-green eyes beneath those thick lashes, not a drop of makeup on her skin, and she's the most stunning woman I've ever seen. Her tight little body, hot as hell in her little dresses or in one of my t-shirts. I picture the way she looked, sprawled out on that bed underneath me yesterday. The way her skin smelled like lavender. Her short, dark hair splayed out behind her. The way her nails dug into my arms, her legs wrapping tighter and tighter around me.

I close my eyes, imagining her tight little body wrapped around me. I picture tugging her little jeans down, just low enough for me to be able to get to my destination. I pump my hand faster and faster, picturing her shoving her head back into the mattress as I work my magic. Then I pull them down a little farther, and—*errrrrrrr. Errrrrrr. Errrrrrrr.* My goddamn phone vibrates around on my nightstand.

"*Fuck,*" I groan as I sigh, reaching for it.

"Hey, Keat," I say.

"Hey," he says. "Did I catch you workin' out?"

I close my eyes, trying to slow down my breathing. Fucking embarrassing.

"Just a warm-up," I say. "What's up?"

"You still want to get breakfast?"

"Yeah, yeah," I say. "What time?"

"I want to be wheels up by eleven. I have some shit to do at home tonight. Can you meet in an hour?"

I look at the clock. Eight a.m.

"No problem. Need me to send a car for you?"

"Nah, I'll walk," he says. "Dino's?"

I smile. Some things never change.

"Dino's. See ya soon."

I get up, put on some shorts and sneakers, and walk down the stairs and through the apartment to my gym. I get through a quick lift, do a few sprints down the turf I had installed, and take the fastest shower known to man. Then I'm out the door with Tyler, on my way down to the car. I look down at my phone, but there's nothing there, and I should be embarrassed at the way I can't stop hoping she will text me.

Normally, I'm not shy about it, but she's with her mom.

I get to Dino's and park around the back. Marlo, Dino's son who owns the place now, spots us and opens the kitchen door. I give him a hug.

"Happy Thanksgiving, brother," he says with a hearty hug. Dino used to keep the place open late for my dad and his associates back in the day. My dad used to pay him to keep the food coming, letting Dino make more in one night than he'd make in a weekend. My dad is not all bad. He just doesn't know it.

When Dino died, Marlo took over, and his relationship with my brothers and me resembles that of our fathers'. My brothers left, but Dino and I stayed close. Some nights, I'll have Tyler or Russ drive my down here for a quiet dinner alone, after most of the city has gone home. It's a tiny little Italian place that has four tables. Most of their business is done at the deli counter. During COVID, Marlo discounted everything on his menu. He made breakfast free for healthcare workers, and paid people who had lost their jobs to deliver food to his vulnerable patrons. I had heard a mysterious donor paid his rent for three years after that. Never confirmed it, though.

"Just you today?" Marlo says, bringing me a hot pot of coffee and my favorite chocolate breakfast pastry he makes. I shake my head.

"Got a special guest today, Marlo," I say just as the bell dings. Marlo looks up, his thick black eyebrows jumping up.

"Keaty!" he shouts, running to my brother and

picking him up. Keaton grunts as Marlo squeezes him, and I see him laugh as he pats his back.

"Happy Thanksgiving, Marlo," he says as he sets him back down. "It's good to see you."

He sits down as Marlo has his staff bring a spread, all our favorite dishes that we have ordered throughout the years, shooting the shit as he goes back and forth. Finally, my brother and I have a few minutes to ourselves.

"So," he says, taking a sip of his coffee and looking up at me through his big dark eyes, "who was the girl?"

I smile and shake my head, taking a sip of my own.

"Not you too, Keat," I say with a chuckle. He laughs and shrugs. I look up at him. I want to tell him—I really do. I want to get this off my chest. Let someone else sit with it. Figure out what the fuck this is. But I can't. "I can't, Keat," I say. His eyebrows shoot up as he chews his hashbrowns.

"Damn," he says.

"What?"

"Brooks the Gossip Queen isn't even here. Just me, and you still won't spill. She must be special," he says. I smile, but it runs away from my face quickly. I clear my throat.

Fuck. She's special.

"I don't know, Keat. I don't know what's going on," I say. "If the time is right, I'll tell you."

He nods and smiles.

"If the time is right," he says with a smile.

The rest of breakfast is good. We're full and stuffed, and Keaton has spent the last twenty minutes telling me about a new sustainable energy startup he's planning to fund this year in California. My brother is so noble. He took his freedom as the second born, and he ran with it. He ran with it in the complete opposite direction as my father did. As I did. And I envy him that. I'm so proud of him.

We say our goodbyes, and he promises to make time to come back over Christmas. And just as I get back in the car, my phone vibrates. When I see her name, I melt. I fumble the phone as I am trying to open it so quickly.

I'm on the beach with my mom in November. Thank you again.

I smile. But I wish she'd stop thanking me.

Hope it's going well. She leaves tonight?

Unfortunately, she types back, as if my people weren't the ones who bought her ticket.

Do you ladies have any dinner plans?

There's a pause, and I feel myself get nervous.

Nothing in particular. We were just going to grab a sandwich on the way to the airport.

How about I take you two out, and we can drop her off together? I type back.

We'd love to.

I can't contain my smile.

See you around four?

We'll be ready.

SAWYER

I am careful during the day while I'm with Mom not to bring Julian up. I revel in the conversation when she does, but I need to be careful. She knows me too well, and her intuition is too good. If she so much as catches a whiff of something going on between Julian and me—not that I even know what that thing would be—I'll never hear the end of it, and any interaction between the three of us will be insanely awkward.

She and I walk to my favorite deli in town in the morning for bagels, walk down to the beach, and go back to the apartment. We read for a few hours in silence, and as much as I can't wait to see Julian, I know that the closer we are to being with him, the closer I am to my mom going away again. Being apart from her like this over the last three years has been such a weight on my heart. A weight that he's helped to lighten over this last month.

But finally, four o'clock rolls around, and I'm trying to act casual while I excuse myself to check myself one last time before he comes. I get ready to look down at my phone when I hear a knock on the door.

I grab my coat as she's grabbing hers and walk toward the door. I pull it open, expecting to see Tyler or Russ, and my stomach flips at the sight of him. Even in jeans and a t-shirt, he makes me completely fucking weak. His face is scruffy, which I love, and his hair is a little more free than normal. I love seeing him like this because he feels so...normal. He feels like Julian. Not Julian Everett.

"Hi," he says with that panty-dropping half-smile as he leans up against the doorway. My mom squeals from around the corner as she approaches, throwing her arms up as I move out of her way and let her get to him. She throws her arms around his neck as he scoops her up, squeezing her right back. "Emily, hi!" he says, and he sounds genuinely excited. He lifts her gently off the ground before setting her back down. Then he gives me a look.

"Oh, hey," he says casually with a flippant wave and a coy smile. My mom laughs as I roll my eyes. But secretly, I love it. I love how familiar he feels to me. How close we feel. "Shall we go?" He holds an arm out toward the door, and he grabs my mom's coat from her and helps her put it on. She walks out into the hallway as I pull one arm in my own, but I stop when I feel his hand grab the other sleeve. He helps me into it then bends forward so his lips are at my ear.

"I'd much rather help you take something *off,*" he whispers then pecks my cheek and walks around me to hold the door. I feel my cheeks flush as I breeze by him out into the hallway where my mother is blissfully unaware of anything going on behind her as she walks toward the steps. I hear him close my door, then I hear him pacing toward us, following us down to the first floor. Outside, Tyler is waiting next to the Escalade, smiling when he sees us. He opens the door, and I climb all the way to the back again so my mother and Julian can take the middle.

And for the next two hours, I can't remember the last time I've felt this happy. I'm with my absolute favorite human being and this man who has quickly become so important to me. It's terrifying and wonderful at the same time. He takes us to Tilly's, the same restaurant he took me to last week. He orders all kinds of food, two bottles of wine, and some delicious desserts. He asks my mom about our family, her upbringing, and being a single mom. I don't talk much. I just sit back and watch them, smiling like a buffoon.

"And then *this* happened, huh?" he asks, jerking his thumb in my direction. I playfully push him as we all laugh, but I watch my mom's eyes change as she looks at me.

"Yep, *that* happened. And it has been the greatest honor of my life." I see her eyes are getting glassy, and I reach out across the table and squeeze her hand. "It's been the two of us since day one, hey, chickadee?" I smile and nod again as she looks back to Julian. "My parents disowned me when I got pregnant. Sawyer's dad left a few months after I got pregnant and never came back. No one was with me when I had her. No one except—"

"Nurse Suzy," we both say in unison. I look at Julian. "Suzy was a labor and delivery nurse working the night I was born. She realized my mom was all alone, so once her shift was over, she stayed three more hours until I was born so my mom wouldn't be alone. We still keep in touch with her to this day."

"We sure do," my mom says. "She was just a stranger who saw someone who needed a person. Sort of like someone else I know." She looks at Julian, and I can sense how uncomfortable he is.

"I was just in the right place at the right time," he says after he clears his throat, looking from her to me. "Sawyer is the one who saved me."

Now *I* am uncomfortable.

"Well, no matter how it happened," my mother says, "I'm just so glad you could both be there for each other when you were."

Julian and I look at each other for a moment then both drop our gazes. We talk for a little while longer before my mother checks the time on her phone.

"Time to go?" Julian asks, and she nods with a sad smile. He pays the bill, and Tyler pulls up outside. The ride to the airport is quiet as I try to calm my anxiety and come to terms with the idea of being separated from her again. But as we pull into JFK, Tyler turns out of the departures lane and onto another driveway. We pull up to a gate, and he shows his ID to a security guard who then lifts it. And before we know it, we're pulling directly onto the tarmac. There are planes driving by, some taking off, one landing, as Tyler drives farther away from the building itself. And as we slow down, I see a beautiful white jet in front of us as he parks a few yards away from it. We look at each other then to Julian, and he smiles.

"The jet is free tonight," he says. "I thought maybe you might enjoy some extra leg room."

My jaw drops as my mother squeals, leaping across the seat to hug him again.

"Julian, oh my, are you sure? The first-class ticket was just fine. This is so much," she says. He nods.

"It's my pleasure. A few of our executives are coming out this week for meetings anyway, so two birds with one stone. Please, enjoy. The crew can whip up all kinds of things, and there is a bed at the back in case you want to rest. Full Wi-Fi too, so you can text a certain, uh, chickadee, if you feel so inclined."

He smiles, she smiles, and I can't stop staring at him in awe. We get out, and Tyler goes to grab her bags, but Julian stops him and takes them from him. He offers her his arm as he leads her to the plane with me following behind. I know it's extra, but I love seeing my mom so happy, seeing her be spoiled the way she deserves to be. She says goodbye to him and thanks him for the millionth time, then she hugs me for a long time, but not long enough.

"I'm going to miss you, chickadee," she whispers as she kisses me again.

"I love you, Mama," I whisper back. She looks at Julian.

"You'll get her home safe?" she asks him. He nods.

"Always," he says, and I know he means it. And finally, we're waving goodbye through the window of the jet as the plane pulls out toward the runway.

We get back in the car, and it's quiet for a few minutes.

"Thank you, Julian," I say just above a whisper. He looks at me then swipes his thumb across my hand, sending chills down my spine.

"Don't thank me, Sawyer," he says, his eyes on mine. We just look at each other for a few moments, taking each other in. *God* I want him. I want to crawl across the seat, into his lap, and finish what he started at Bedell House. I want to show him how grateful I am to him. I want to show him how badly I want him, like I've never wanted anyone. I'm having images of us rolling around the penthouse, breaking vases, tearing each other's clothes off. But before I know it, we're pulling back onto my street. And then he's helping me out of the car and walking me back up to my door.

I give him my best "fuck me" look. I bite my lip. I bat my eyelashes. I thank him again. I reach for his arm, squeezing it. He bends down, and I hold my breath. But instead, he leaves a long, soft kiss on my forehead.

"Goodnight, Sawyer," he says, opening the door and nudging me inside.

I clear my throat, feeling my loins sizzle like they've been doused in freezing-cold water.

"Goodnight," I mumble before I slam the door shut.

SAWYER

I don't waste time stripping off my jeans and pulling on his t-shirt. I wash my face and grab my book, nestling into my favorite corner of the couch. But I can't concentrate on a damn word I'm reading. Because all I want is him.

And I'm furious about it.

I pull out my phone.

I think about sending him a strongly worded text about how he needs to stop messing with my head. But instead, I decide on a selfie that's half my face and half his shirt. Without giving myself time to reconsider, I send it, biting my lip. I throw my phone on the couch, telling myself I'm not going to check it. But when I hear it vibrate, I practically pull my own arm out the socket trying to reach for it.

Nice shirt. Looks better on you.

Thanks, I say. *It's my new nighttime go-to.*

Oh yeah? What do you wear with it?

I pause, my stomach turning.

Nothing, I write back before I can overthink it.

But to my dismay, there is no response. Not in one minute. Not in five. Not in fourteen. I've bit my thumbnail down to the quick, my leg bouncing so hard I'm making an imprint in the carpet.

Finally, when I can't take the anxiety anymore, I go to get up. But as I do, I'm startled by a loud banging on my door.

I freeze.

Bang, bang, bang. I swallow, tiptoeing across the living room to the door. I look through the peephole, and my stomach turns again.

Oh, my god.

I unlock it and open it slowly, hiding my bottom half behind the door as I look up at him. I was emboldened by my libido and the safety of being a few miles away from him. But now he's here.

He stares down at me, his hair slightly disheveled, with this look in his eye that I only saw yesterday in that bedroom. A look that's equally as pained as it is determined. A look like he's having an internal argument, and he doesn't know which side he should let win. But he pushes the door open, stepping inside, and closes it. He takes my arm, pulling me gently so I'm in front of him.

"Don't go hiding now," he says, then his lips crash into mine, his arms snaking around my body as he lifts me off the ground. I wrap my legs around his waist as one of his hands slides up and down one of them, the other cupping my ass as he carries me to the kitchen and sets me on the counter.

He picks me up again, spinning me around and carrying me toward the couch. He moves a pillow and lays me down gently, kissing me softly, then more urgently, then soft again as he situates me on the couch.

"I love how it looks on you," he says between kisses as his hands slide up and down my freshly shaved legs, "but I want to see it off of you." I moan lightly against his lips as his hands slide up past my hips, over my panties, toward my stomach.

And then I become aware of everything that's transpiring. I've gotten so used to him being the strong one, the one who stops it before it gets to a point of no return, that I don't know how to act when that point never comes. I push up against him, pushing him toward the back of the couch as I crawl up onto my knees and straddle him.

"You said you didn't know what you wanted from me," I whisper. He looks up at me, his eyebrows knitting together. He reaches a hand up, caressing my cheek before wrapping his hand through my hair.

"I don't. I don't know what any of this is," he says. "But I know that I don't want anyone else to have you. And I don't want any part of anyone else."

Oh, fuck.

"Prove it," I say, a sly little smile playing on my lips. He smiles and shakes his head, pulling me down to him. I slide back and forth on his lap while he kisses me, my own wetness seeping through the silk of my panties and onto him.

He pushes to his feet, still holding me to him, carrying me into the bedroom. He lays me down gently, his hand under my head. Slowly, we come apart as his hands find the bottom of my—well, his— shirt, and I swallow. He pulls the fabric up slowly, and I feel chills ripple across my skin. Finally, he tugs it off over my head, and I lie there, almost naked, in front of Julian Everett. He tugs off his own shirt, and I ogle at the body I've spent an embarrassing number of hours stalking on the internet. But *God*, it's so much better in person.

He unzips his jeans, kicking them off. I push up onto my elbows, then I sit all the way up. He stands in front of me, and I reach out and pull him closer by the waistband of his boxers. I tug them gently, looking up at him to make sure he's okay with it. He nods slowly, stroking my hair as I pull them down, letting him spring free.

Oh. So that's *a penis.* I don't know what the fraternity brothers I let hit it for the last few years were working with, but it was *nothing* like this. It's long and thick with a snake-like vein running down the shaft and a tuft of trimmed brown hair at the top.

It's *beautiful.*

"Your turn, honey," he says, pushing me back gently. I swallow as he reaches up, hooking his thumbs under the straps and pulling them down. And then he's staring down at me, *all* of me. "My god, Sawyer. You are beautiful."

I swallow again as the heat flushes in my cheeks. He kneels down toward me, as I push up on my elbows again, kissing me softly. He pauses, holding my chin in his hand.

"I'm going to ruin you, sweetheart," he whispers. I bring my lips to his again, letting my tongue invade his mouth, biting gently on his bottom lip.

"I wish you'd do it faster," I say. His eyes jump, alighting with a fire I haven't seen yet. And then, it's like a beast has been unleashed. He kisses me again, sliding one hand down to my neck, then between my breasts, down to my pussy. When his fingers slide between my folds and he feels how wet I am, a low moan escapes his lips that makes me want to erupt like a fucking geyser.

"Oh, honey," he whispers, "you're ready for me, huh?"

I nod.

"I've been ready," I say.

"Mmm," he moans again. He moves his hand in a slow circle at first, pressing against my clit with just the right amount of pressure before he slips two fingers inside of me. I press my head back into the mattress, clutching at the blankets.

"Sweetheart?"

"Hmm?"

"I'm going to taste you now," he says.

Oh, fuck.

I nod slowly, closing my eyes as our lips part, and he moves down my body, leaving little kisses all over my skin as he does.

When he gets to my center, he wraps a hand around either of my legs. He drags his lips down my inner thighs, leaving a trail of heat in their wake. Then he pushes my legs up and apart, leaving me open and exposed and throbbing for more.

His eyes flick up to me for a moment, then he dives in. He drags his tongue up and down my slit. He uses his thumbs to spread me apart more, pushing his face farther and farther into me as his tongue pulses against me, the orgasm building in my belly.

"Honey, I could eat you out all goddamn day," he says. "You are fucking delicious."

"Oh, Julian," I whimper, one hand clutching the blanket, the other grasping for the back of his head. I press him deeper into me, wishing I could keep him there forever as he moves his head in all the right directions. "Oh, God," I cry as he sucks my whole clit into his mouth, massaging it with his tongue as he does. Just when I feel like I'm on the brink, I feel him slip a finger back in, then another. And then they all move in perfect harmony: his tongue, his fingers, pulsing and stroking and sucking until I'm screaming his name, moaning, shuddering like a fool on the bed.

My chest heaves with heavy breaths as he slowly rises, pulling his fingers out of me and sticking them into his own mouth, sucking my juices off them. I've never seen something this earth-shatteringly sexy before, but I'm pretty sure I can die a happy woman.

"Oh, my god," I whisper. He stands up, and I gather enough strength to sit up in front of him. "It's my turn," I tell him, and never have I ever wanted to suck someone's cock so bad. I want him as deep as I can take him. I want to choke on him. I want him to see the tears in my eyes, knowing I'm doing as much as I can for him. He looks down at me, and I spin around on my back, lying down so that my head hangs off the bed.

"Fuck my mouth, Julian," I tell him, and I hear him hiss as he gently grabs a fistful of my hair.

"Sawyer," he warns. "You need to watch that pretty little mouth of yours. You're supposed to be young and innocent. We don't want to mess that up too bad, do we?"

I reach a hand back, cupping his balls and stroking his cock with the other. Then I tilt my head back and open my mouth wide. He smiles for a moment then reaches his other hand out to grab the other side of my head. He pushes his cock into my mouth slowly, and the salty taste of his precum has my insides swirling for more. I reach my hands back and grab his ass, pulling him farther and farther into my mouth.

I swallow and adjust to his size, then I feel him stroke my face.

"You're doing so good, sweetheart," he says. "Are you ready?"

I nod beneath him, and he starts to move. He goes

slowly at first, but when I squeeze and dig my nails into his ass, he picks up the pace. I'm gagging and choking in the most glorious way while he hisses above me, gently pulling my hair as I clutch onto him. My eyes fill with tears, and all I want now is for him to lose it. I want him to completely fucking—

All of a sudden, he freezes, slowing down and holding me slightly off of him.

"Honey, if we don't stop right now, there won't be another chance before your mouth is full."

SAWYER

*D*ear God. *That's all I want.* My mouth fills with more saliva as I dig my nails deeper into him. He hisses as he rubs the sides of my head gently.

"No, baby," he says. "Not like this. Not this time."

God dammit.

He pulls out of my mouth and bends down, kissing me gently before reaching up and spinning me around.

"You," he says, putting a hand down on either side of my head and wiping the last tear from my eye, "are *very* good at that."

I smile and swipe my thumb over my lips.

He stares down at me as he grabs himself, pumping his hand up and down a few times. I take in every single inch of him—the patch of hair on his big broad chest, the veins snaking down his arms, his hair falling out of place, the way every muscle in his body ripples when he moves—and I don't ever want to forget a single detail. I reach up, wrapping my hands around his thick forearms.

He reaches over to the nightstand and opens the drawer. He sees the box of condoms and grabs it, but as he pulls one out, he pauses, lifting his eyes to me.

"What?" I ask.

"I'm glad you have these," he says, "but I also really fucking hate that you have these."

I swallow.

I kind of love that he's jealous over me.

"Tell me again," I say as he puts one on then climbs onto the bed. He gently reaches for my legs, spreading them apart.

"Tell you what, honey?"

"Tell me what you said earlier. About what you want," I say.

He bends down, kissing me gently but nibbling on my bottom lip before he comes up.

"I don't want anyone else to have you," he says, kissing my neck, his hand sliding down to my breast and circling it. "And I don't want anyone else." Then he pulls my legs, sliding me down toward him, and pushes himself into me. I cry out, my legs wrapping around him as I clutch onto his head and shoulders. "Are you okay, baby?"

I nod, evening out my breathing and taking him in. I'm feeling him in places I didn't know were reachable by anyone other than my gynecologist.

"I'll go slow," he whispers, moving in and out of me as he holds himself over me. When I've adjusted to him more, he reaches down and hooks a hand under one of my legs, throwing it up over his shoulder. He scoots closer to me on his knees then brings the other one up, picking up the pace. The angle makes my eyes roll back into my head, and I claw at the sheets like I'm rabid.

"Julian!" I scream out, and he tightens his grip on me, moving faster and faster. He spreads my legs slightly, reaching down and putting the pads of his fingers on my clit and moving them over and over. Just as I'm feeling like I'm going to explode, he pulls out of me, taking my soul with him. He flips me around so that I'm on my stomach, pressing me down and pulling my ass up to him. He bends down and kisses my right ass cheek then pushes himself back into me from behind. As he starts going again, he reaches a hand around, pulling me up so that his chest is to my back. Then his hand moves back down to my clit as he circles it, pounding in and out of me. I lay my head back against his shoulder, wrapping an arm around him.

"Julian," I puff. "Julian..."

He groans in my ear, his breathing erratic as he moves. And then, everything goes white. Stars fill my eyes as my whole body shakes against his. He wraps his arm around my middle, holding me steady to him as I sink all my weight back. Our bodies are slick with sweat, sticking to each other. He kisses my shoulder then my neck before slowly pulling out of me.

The aftershock rolls through me as he climbs off

the bed and goes to the bathroom. He's back a moment later, and my stomach starts to churn. What happens now?

I pull the covers up to my chest, lying on the bed as he pulls his boxers on. He looks at me as he walks toward the bed, and I brace myself for what's next.

"Can I stay?" he asks. I can't help but smile, as childlike as it might make me look.

"You pay the rent," I say. "Of course you can stay."

He smiles as he gets in the bed, pulling the covers up onto both of us. He snakes an arm underneath me and pulls me into him, spooning me and burying his face in the back of my neck.

I know I have him in this moment, but I don't know for how long.

And the problem is, now that I've had him, I don't want to let him go.

We lie still for a few moments with nothing but the moon lighting up the room.

"What is it, Sawyer?" he asks, and I feel myself get stiff. I clear my throat.

"What do you mean?" I ask. He sighs, flipping me over so I'm facing him on the pillow.

"Tell me what's got your heart rate going like we never finished," he says. *Fuck.* Am I that easy of a read, or does he just know me?

I bite my lip, and he reaches a hand up, caressing my cheek and tucking my hair behind my ear.

"What...what happens now?" I ask. His eyebrows knit together as his eyes narrow on me.

"What do you mean?"

I clear my throat.

"Do we just...I mean, are we...what does this..."

"I meant what I said, Sawyer. I don't want anyone else to have you, and I don't want anyone else. What about you?"

It's almost laughable. Is he asking *me* if I want to be exclusive? With the gorgeous billionaire hero I haven't gone a minute without thinking about since we met?

"I don't want anyone else either," I say. He smiles. "But...but you said you don't do relationships. You don't—"

"I don't," he says. "I never have. But I've never had someone...anyone in my life who sees me like you do, Sawyer. And I can't seem to let you go."

I feel a lump in my throat.

"So..."

"But it's complicated, Sawyer. I can't have a normal relationship. So if we were to do this, you would have to decide how you want things to be."

"What do you mean?"

"I mean that if we are together, the world will know. If we go to dinner anywhere but Tilly's or Dino's, the world will know. My family will know. People on the internet will know. And they will have things to say about it. In an hour's time, they'll know your name, where you're from, where you go to school, your mother's name. They'll know how we met. They'll dig into the shooting. Look, I've never told a soul about you—not even my brothers. And it's not because I'm ashamed or because I'm being sneaky. Honey, I'd proudly show you off to the whole damn world. Happily get the grilling from my brothers about being a cradle robber. But if I do that, everything changes, Sawyer. And it can't go back." I swallow, pushing myself up to lean against the headboard. I tuck the covers around myself tighter, losing myself in thought. "I want you, Sawyer. I don't even know what this looks like. I've never wanted this before. But I can't hurt you. I won't. So it has to be what *you* want."

God, it would be nice to see this through. The way he makes me feel like the only girl on the planet, even when he has the whole planet at his fingertips. The way he feels like home. But I enjoy my time in the dark. Sometimes, it's nice not being seen.

And my mom...it wouldn't just affect me.

He pulls himself up, wrapping his arms around me and bringing my head to his chest. He kisses the top of my head, gently scratching my scalp.

"Sweetheart, you don't have to decide any of this tonight. Or tomorrow. Or the next day." He pulls away and looks down at me. "Besides, there are some things you need to know about my family before you tie yourself to me in any way publicly. So take your time. I'm in this until you say you want out...for as long as it takes."

I smile up at him, and he leans down to kiss me. Of course I am absolutely *dying* to know what he's talking about. But I also don't want this moment to end. So for once, I keep my mouth shut.

"Want some French toast?" he asks me. I raise an eyebrow, and he laughs.

"What?" I giggle. "Is that your post-sex go-to?"

He shrugs.

"I don't know," he says. "I've never stayed after before."

My eyes widen as he kisses me again then scoots off the bed and out the door.

I sigh as I listen to him humming in the kitchen, opening the silverware drawer then the fridge.

I'd give anything to stay here, just like this, in this apartment, never having to share him with the world again.

JULIAN

I made us French toast at midnight, we took a long, hot shower where I bent her over and took her again, and then we got into her little bed and watched *Cheers* until she fell asleep, curled up against me. And now, I've just been lying here for the last hour or so, watching her take long breaths in and out, that little furrow that's always in her brow finally relaxed. Her wet hair soaks my skin, but I don't care. I'd rather lose my arm than wake her.

I stroke my thumb gently against her face, smiling as she breathes.

Fuck. This feels...big.

For the first time in my adult life, I feel excited about the idea of being with someone. I feel this connection to her that I've never felt with anyone else.

In a month's time, she's spun my world on its axis. She's made me see this whole possibility of a life beyond the business, beyond the name. That I can find more joy in a spaghetti dinner or in pillow talk as I do traveling the world or buying businesses.

And for the first time in my adult life...I'm terrified of losing someone. I didn't want to bring all of that up. I don't want to scare her. God knows I'm hoping she will be game for the insanity that is being connected to the Everett name, but I also care too much for her to let her go in blind. I've never known life to be different than this. There were cameras outside of the hospital the day I was born, and my grandfather sued one newspaper and bought another out of spite for publishing photos of me.

But I've seen the way it works for people that come in or become affiliated with us. I've watched the way the press has torn apart my mother. I've watched the way innocent people who have barely scratched the surface of our lives have never really regained their own after whatever tryst they have had with us. And what I said is true...when it happens, it can't be undone. They're tied to us in infamy while we move on with grace and wonder in the eyes of the world. It's fucked up, and it's unfair. When I had a few relationships in my twenties, I did everything I could to protect my partners and keep a sense of confidentiality. But each time, it ended up being in vain when they would decide to throw themselves to the wolves in order to hold on to whatever shred of fame being with me brought them.

But with her, it's different.

She doesn't see me as Julian the Billionaire. I mean, she certainly sees the money. But she doesn't expect it. She doesn't take it for granted. And the best part is, she could do without it. If we spent every night in the little dorm room I once rescued her from, she'd be just as content as she would be in my penthouse. She has survival instincts that I am very aware that I will never have. And it makes her impenetrable in ways that I've never experienced. She's sixteen years younger than I am, and in some ways, she's lived so much more than I have.

I don't want to lose her.

I can't lose her.

But there are some things that money can't buy, and Sawyer is definitely one of them.

WHEN I WAKE up the next morning, she's staring at me. I can't help but chuckle at her big green eyes, long lashes batting in my direction.

"You are so pretty," she says, and I laugh out loud.

"Good morning to you too," I say, "and...what?"

She smiles and shrugs.

"You are. If you have all the money in the world and, like, own continents or whatever, you should have to be ugly. It should be a rule," she says. I laugh out loud again, pulling her into me and kissing her hard. "I've been waiting for you to wake up."

"Oh, yeah?" I ask, rubbing my eyes. She nods then

bites her lip. Then she slips down under the covers and yanks my boxers down. I jump and reach for her arms, but I'm in her mouth before I can make another move.

She moans as my precum spills out into her mouth, slurping and swallowing and making me spiral as she does. She digs her nails into my ass then uses one hand to cup my balls before she wraps her long fingers around my cock.

"Fuck, Sawyer," I grunt as she takes me deeper, gagging as I get dangerously close to the back of her throat. I feel myself growing harder and thicker with every suck, and I instinctively take a handful of her hair, gently fisting it as she moves.

"S-Sawyer, Sawyer," I say, tapping her arms and loosening my grip on her hair. She comes up, flipping the blanket off her and wiping her mouth then the tears pooling in her eyes.

"What's wrong?" she asks. I shake my head.

"Nothing at all, but if you didn't stop, your mouth was going to be full," I say, stroking her cheek. She raises one eyebrow, looking at me.

"That was sort of the point," she says. Now I raise an eyebrow at her.

"You want that?" I ask. She makes a face at me and crosses her arms over her chest.

"If I didn't want that, I probably wouldn't have started my day by putting your dick in my mouth," she says. I chuckle again.

"Putting my dick in your mouth and getting me *off*

in your mouth are two different things, sweetheart," I tell her. She crosses her arms tighter over her chest.

"I'm aware," she says, her lips pursed. Suddenly, I feel this green rage building inside of me. I grip her hips.

"So you've done that before?" I ask, my voice low and husky.

Her eyes narrow on me as she bites the inside of her lip. She looks as if she's slightly afraid to answer the question but also that she wants to see how I react.

"Many times," she says. Then she leans forward, putting one hand on my chest and pushing me back down. "Is that a problem? You wanna keep talking about all the other guys I've gone down on, or may I continue?"

I push up, gripping the back of her head and pulling her to me. I kiss her hard and possessively, my tongue plunging into her mouth. The thought of her doing this with anyone else has every muscle in my body tensing up and my fists clenching.

"Knees," I say. "Now."

Her eyes dance with excitement as she scrambles off the bed, tucking her hair behind her ears as I scoot to the edge.

"Thattagirl," I say as she opens her mouth, guiding me back in. I hiss as she takes me deep, making up for lost time. I grip her hair again, watching as she moves up and down my shaft. She gags, and I hiss again, her eyes flying open. "Do you need to stop, baby?"

She looks up at me, eyes filling with tears, but she digs her nails into my legs and shakes her head no.

I cock my head as I stroke her face.

"Can you handle this load, sweetheart?" I ask. She nods slowly as she speeds up her movements, pausing every now and then to circle my head with her tongue before taking all of me into her mouth again. "You're doing so good, sweetheart. I'm...I'm almost there," I hiss, scooting farther off the bed and deeper into her mouth. I pull her head to me gently, dropping my head back as her hand moves up to cradle my balls again, and that's all it takes for me to blow. I fold over, a shudder going through me as I erupt, and she gulps me down, sliding off me slowly and taking in a deep breath. I lean forward, swiping the moisture from the corner of her mouth with my thumb, and then cup her head in my hands, catching my breath for a minute.

"What a perfect, dirty little mouth you have, my girl," I say with a smile as I lean forward and kiss her. "I love how good you are at that, but I *hate* how good you are at that. I tighten my grip on her. "I want you to forget about anyone else you've ever done that to."

She smiles.

"Territorial, are we?"

I pull her in for one last kiss.

"You have no idea."

And the truth is, neither do I. I have never been attached to someone like this, let alone given a shit about who else they'd had in their bed. Or their mouth. The thought of her on her knees for someone else is enough to make me put a hole in the wall. But the thought of someone else pleasuring *her*? Put me in a goddamn asylum.

I know I'm supposed to be giving her time. No pressure. Being with me would be a lot to swallow—pun intended. But the problem is, I'm starting to get scared. The decision is in her hands, and I am terrified that I won't be her choice.

SAWYER

I'm getting way too comfortable waking up next to him. For the last few weeks, either I'm in his bed, or he's in mine. Obviously, I'm not one to complain about waking up in the most expensive penthouse in Manhattan on the regular, with amazing sex at night and professionally cooked meals in the morning. He drives me to my shifts at the mini-mart when I have them and usually arranges his meeting schedule around my pick-ups. Sometimes he takes a meeting from one of our apartments, and I just sit in awe, watching him run the world from the comfort of the pull-out couch he bought me.

I love watching him work. I love how he carries himself. I love listening in on how he treats his employees. Nothing like the ruthless, infamous persona of his father that I've seen on TV, but more gentle. He listens. He asks them questions. He has faith in them.

It's hot.

So far, being "us" hasn't come up again since that one conversation a few weeks ago in my apartment, and if I'm being honest, I'm avoiding it. Because it feels like "us." The way we schedule our lives around each other feels like "us." The way he blows my fucking mind every time we fuck feels like "us." The way he still calls me every night that we don't spend together so that I can fall asleep feels like an "us."

And it's amazing.

And it feels pretty perfect the way it is.

The trouble is that, although it feels like we are together more than not, it still feels like there are a lot of things we *can't* do together. There are the little things, like holding hands in public. And then there are the bigger things, like telling my mom or meeting his family, helping him figure out how to use his fortune for good instead of evil.

That kind of thing.

And then there are the things like the article I came across today, published a few months back, about how he is the most eligible bachelor in the country—or maybe the world—and I want to fight someone.

He's eligible, but as far as I'm concerned, he is *not* available.

And it's up to me whether or not the world knows it.

My world, compared to his, is so small.

A small college campus, a small job, small family, small life.

But there are things about being small that I don't take for granted. Like anonymity.

I like to think that my being a nobody has its perks for him too. No one is looking for the third richest man in the world on the Carrington campus or holed up in my walk-up at night.

We're just a few days away from Christmas, and the only thing keeping me from being devastated about not going home for the whole break this year is him. The semester break is six weeks, and I can't go that long without getting a paycheck, and neither can my mom. So I'm going back for a few days then coming back to Connecticut for the rest of the break. The flight alone will be almost a month's wages for me, and even though I know Julian would pay for it in a heartbeat, I'm very conscious of that line. I will not be someone who expects anything different from him than I would any other partner. Although, any other partner of mine would likely be another poor college student or a trust fund baby who would need permission to spend his daddy's money.

But still.

The few times it's come up, I've just mentioned that we are both working a lot.

He's nodded, and then we've moved on.

I'M in the back of the car, pulling out my phone to text him after my shift. He had a dinner commitment, but he sent Tyler to get me and bring me home.

All done, I say. *On the way home.*

I wish I was too. I hope it was an easy shift.

Only three old men hit on me today. It was a blow to my self-esteem, I write back. He dislikes the message.

You already have one old man hitting on you daily. You don't need anyone else. I'll happily come let them know.

I smile. I love that he has claimed me, even if it's only for me to know.

Be my guest.

WE'RE HOME a few moments later, and Tyler walks me up to the apartment as instructed, waiting until I get inside. I thank him then lock the door and immediately head for the kitchen and my speaker. I start some Kendrick, dancing around the kitchen as I open my embarrassingly empty fridge. I let the music blast as I walk into my bedroom, stripping off my gray polo and jeans and putting on some tiny pajama shorts and a tank top.

I do my signature shuffle-shuffle-slide move back out the door and into the living room, then I freeze when my front door crashes open.

I scream and jump.

A man and a woman—who have very obviously just been hard-core making out—are standing in my doorway, staring at me. All three of us have our jaws to the floor.

I yell at my speaker to shut off as I attempt to cover myself over my see-through silk shirt.

"Who the fuck are you?" I scream, scooting closer to my bedroom. Of course my phone is across the apartment on the counter where I left it. The man gives me a look, raising an eyebrow and slowly taking his hands off the girl who is straightening out her top and wiping her mouth.

"Who the fuck are *you*," the man asks, "and what are you doing in my apartment?"

*N*ow I'm the one giving him the look. I reach around my bedroom door and grab my sweat jacket, putting it on quickly.

"Your apartment?" I ask. "Who are you?" I ask again.

The girl scoffs and clicks her tongue.

"This is Brooks Everett."

My eyes widen. Now I see it. The familiar brown eyes and perfect jawline. Their noses are different—and I much prefer the slight crookedness of *my* Everett's—but I definitely see it.

Fuck.

"Now," he says with an overly confident smirk, "do you mind telling me who you are and how you got in my family's apartment?"

"Fuck," I whisper. I dash to the counter and pick up my phone. He watches every move I make while the tall blonde rolls her eyes and smacks her gum, clicking her heels on the floor every time she alternates sticking one hip out. I dial Julian, biting my lip while I hold the gaze of the youngest Everett brother—funnily enough, the one who I'm closest to in age.

"Hi, baby," he says in a hushed voice. "Everything okay?"

"Yes, I'm sorry. I know you're in a meeting, but, uh...I think we have a problem. Your brother is here."

Brooks's eyes widen as he watches me on the phone.

"Yeah, okay," I say, walking toward him and handing it over.

"So, is this the girl from Bedell House?" he asks, that same smug smile on his face. *Shit. He knows about me?* Or even worse...*was there another girl at Bedell House?* "Uh-huh. Yep, no problem. Oh, don't you worry. I'll wait right here."

I swallow as he hands me the phone back.

"Hello?" I whisper, walking into my room.

"I'm so sorry. I'll be there soon. Hang tight. I'll take care of this," he says. I nod, my heart pounding.

"Okay," I say, having no choice but to do as he says and just sit tight.

When I go back into the living room, Brooks is apologizing and walking the blonde to the door.

"Unreal. Some fucking date," she squeals as she yanks her alligator bag up over her shoulder. "We don't even make it to the fucking restaurant, and now

I'm supposed to just leave you in this janky apartment with some other chick? This is the last fucking time, Brooks," she goes on, stomping across the floor to the door.

"Okay, sweetheart, apologies again." He nods, holding the door open. "Adam is waiting for you downstairs. He will take you wherever you'd like to go. I'm sorry you weren't satisfied with the evening, but feel free to keep the earrings. Remember, you signed the NDA at the start of the night, so none of this can be repeated. It was really great to see you, Candy," he says.

She doesn't say another word, just sticks up a perfectly manicured middle finger in his face and storms off. He chuckles and closes the door behind her, turning to me with a shrug.

"That's the third time she's broken up with me this month," he says.

Gross.

"Well, it's nice to see that the rumors about you hold no merit," I say, walking past him toward the couch and sitting down, pulling the throw over me. I'm hungry, but I feel weird doing anything else in this apartment that may or may not belong to the strange man here with me.

He laughs as he turns to the fridge, helping himself. He grabs two Frescas, the only thing I have to drink around here, and brings them to the living room. He slides one across the coffee table to me then plops down on the oversized chair and puts his feet up on the table.

"I like what you've done with the place," he says. "The new furniture looks good."

I open my can and take a sip, nodding. I don't know what I should and shouldn't say, if anything.

"I don't suppose you're gonna give me much until my brother gets here, huh?" he asks with that same cocky smirk. "How you met? How you ended up here? Your name...?"

Is my name even safe? I have no idea. I have no clue how any of this works.

I just raise my eyebrows then take a long sip of my drink.

After twenty agonizing minutes, the door unlocks, and in walks my billionaire-in-shining-armor.

"There he is," Brooks says as he leans back against the couch. "My wonderful big brother. Keeper of family secrets. Squatter. Professional bullshitter."

Julian shoots him a glare as he closes the door behind him. He kicks off his shoes and waltzes across the apartment. He kicks his brother's feet down off the table, ignoring his quip, and bends down right in front of me.

Before I can say anything, he lays a soft kiss on my lips. He smiles as we come apart, and I instantly feel myself relax.

"Now," he says with a sigh and turning to his brother, "what are you doing here, Brooks?"

Brooks looks to me, then to him, then back to me with that same stupid smile on his face.

"Oh my," Brooks finally says. "This is too good. Oh, no, no, Big Brother. I think it's *your* turn to answer some questions."

Julian sighs again then takes a seat beside me on the couch. He wraps an arm around me and pulls me into him.

"It's okay," he says. "He won't say anything." I nod and swallow nervously. *Here goes nothin'.* He turns back to Brooks. "Ask."

"Where do I start?" he says in amusement, clapping his hands together. "Okay, let's go with...who is she, how'd you meet her, and what is she doing in our apartment?" He opens his hand on my shoulder, and I slip mine into his, locking our fingers together.

"This is Sawyer. Sawyer, meet my idiot brother Brooks," he says, pointing his hand in his brother's direction. I smile and wave.

"Sawyer," Brooks says with a smile and nod.

"We met on the Carrington campus, the day of the shooting," Julian goes on. "I was just arriving for my guest panel when it started. She happened to be running in my direction and stopped us. She saved my life," he says. I squeeze his hand subconsciously, my eyes dropping. Slowly, I look back at Brooks, whose face is much more serious now.

"Fuck," he says. "I'm so sorry."

"Thank you," I say. "Your brother saved me too." He raises an eyebrow, so I go on. "He got me off campus, brought me back to his apartment while campus was locked down, before they caught the guy. I'm from Seattle, so my mom couldn't get here till the next day."

Brooks shakes his head.

"I'm sorry, Sawyer. Glad you were there, Brother," he says. Julian leans over and kisses my temple.

"So am I," he whispers. "Anyhow, we kept in touch. Like she said, her mom doesn't live out here. I wanted to make sure she was okay after everything."

"He's being modest," I interject. "He flew my mom out here to be with me, got us a suite to stay in while campus was closed. And when it reopened, I had some trouble going back to my dorm. My roommate...she, um...she didn't make it," I say, feeling this familiar lump in my throat I've felt so much after these last few weeks. "Your brother...he, uh...he rented this place for me to finish out the semester. Or I guess bought it?" I ask, turning to him.

Julian clears his throat.

"My family owns the building," he says. "This unit was vacant. I knew you'd try to fight me, so I made up the lease thing. I'm sorry."

I smile and bring his fingers to my lips. How could I be mad?

"I'm sorry about your friend, Sawyer. I really am. And I'm really fucking sorry that you went through that," Brooks says. His face is sincere, and I smile.

"Thank you, Brooks."

"So this..." he says, motioning between us, "turned

into a little something more than 'making sure she was okay,' huh?"

"It did," Julian says. "We're still figuring some things out—well, she is."

Brooks raises an eyebrow again, and so do I.

"As far as I'm concerned, I'm all hers, and she's all mine. But we're doing things on her time. As you know, once she decides it's time to tell the world, there's no going back."

He's talking to his brother, but he's saying it to me. I'm staring at him while he speaks with so much conviction, like professing his feelings for me is the most natural thing in the world. I slowly become aware that we are not alone again and turn back to Brooks, who has a surprised look on his face. He lets out a sharp whistle.

"Well damn, Brother," he says, slapping his knee. "I never thought I'd see the day. And listen, I'm happy for you both. Really, I am. My lips are sealed. He stands up slowly, and Julian and I follow suit. He pulls Julian in for a long hug, patting his back, and I can see that he means it. Then he reaches around and hugs me tight too. "Be good to him, Sawyer," he whispers in my ear. Then he pulls back. "It was great to meet you. Hope to see more of you. Big Brother, I'll talk to you soon."

He claps Julian's back, and then he walks back out the door.

I turn slowly to Julian, my eyes big and my heart pounding.

"I'm sorry, baby," he says, reaching out to take my hands in his. "I had no idea he was still using this place as his...I don't know. And I don't want to know," he chuckles. "But I'm sorry. I promise he won't say anything, though."

I bite my lip.

"Did you mean what you told him?" I ask. My heart is thudding so hard in my chest that it feels like it's moving my whole body. He pulls me into him slightly, wrapping one arm around my waist and putting the other palm on my cheek. His eyebrows knit together as his big brown eyes bore into mine.

"Yes, sweetheart," he says. "Every word. If you want me, I'm yours." I swallow, then I tuck my arms inside of his and wrap them around him.

"It felt good, telling someone," I admit. His perfect lips tug into a half-smile as he looks down at me.

"Oh, yeah?" he asks.

"Mm-hmm," I say. "Even if he thinks you're my sugar daddy, which I guess you kind of are."

He laughs, bending down to leave a string of soft kisses under my ear, down my jawline.

"I do kind of like you calling me 'Daddy.' But I'll be whatever you want me to be," he says. "However you want me to be it."

Chills erupt all over my skin from his touch.

I want this. Every day. With him and only him.

"I don't want anyone else to have you, Julian," I whisper. "And I want everyone to know that they can't have you." He stops kissing me, our eyes locking as he stands up. He cocks an eyebrow, trying to decide if I'm saying what he thinks I'm saying.

"What...what are you saying, Sawyer?" he asks.

"I'm saying that I'm all in," I tell him. "I want you, and I want this. I don't want to sneak around anymore."

Slowly, the intense look on his face eases up. His eyebrows smooth out, and his face breaks out into the biggest smile I have ever seen. He pulls me in for a long, hard kiss, scooping me up off the ground as he slides one hand under my ass and slides one up my back into my hair. I wrap my legs around him as he carries me through the apartment and into the bedroom.

We come apart for a moment, and he closes his eyes, pressing his forehead to mine.

"I don't think I realized how badly I wanted to hear you say those words until you actually did," he says. I smile, running my fingers through his brown waves and kissing his forehead.

"I've been wanting to say them for a while," I tell him. He stares up at me, still holding me up.

"There are still some things I want to tell you before we make any moves," he says. I smile, bending down to kiss him again.

"Okay," I say. "But could that wait?"

"Wait for what?"

"Wait until after you fuck me like you don't want anyone else to," I say. I feel his cock twitch beneath me.

"Oh, baby," he growls as he spins me around, carrying me to the bed and laying me down on top of it. "I'm gonna fuck you so that you don't remember any other man that's ever touched you. And so you never want to be touched by anyone else ever again."

JULIAN

I'm not sure if it's the adrenaline from having to save her from my family, the way it felt to be professing my devotion to her out loud, the fact that she wants it in return, or an explosive combination, but I need her *yesterday*.

She's got on a cute little button-up night shirt with plaid pajama shorts that show off the little curve of her ass. An ass that my pigheaded little brother was undoubtedly enjoying before I got here. Probably after too.

I lay her down gently on the bed, kissing her wildly while my hands travel down her sides.

"Sweetheart?" I ask.

"Mmm?" is all she can muster up.

"You know I care about you, right?" I ask. She nods, her eyebrows knitting together. I kiss her lips. "You know I'd do anything to keep you safe?" Her eyebrows tug tighter, but she nods again. "And you know I have nothing but the utmost respect and highest opinion of you, right?"

"Why are you asking me all of this?" she asks.

"Because in a second, the things I'm going to do to you might say otherwise."

Her lips tug up into a devious little smile, and she bites her bottom one.

"Get going, then," she says, and I do. I reach for the sides of her shirt, tearing it open and making buttons fly in every direction.

"I'll buy you a new one," I say, and she giggles as the shirt falls to her sides, her breasts spilling out.

I grab one, holding it taut and lunging for it, sucking it into my mouth and swirling my tongue around her nipple. She lets out a little whimper beneath me that makes me feral, and I switch and grab the other one. I kiss between them and down her stomach to the hemline of her shorts as I raise my eyes to hers.

"Tell me again," I command.

"Tell you what?" she asks, her voice breathy.

"Tell me that you want this. That you want us."

"I want *you*," she moans. "I'm all in."

It's enough to put me over the edge. I reach for her shorts, pulling them down with enough force that it makes her gasp. And when I realize she has no panties on, I swear I'm about to blow inside my fucking pants.

"Oh, my bad little girl," I murmur. She smiles, biting her lip, and I slide down farther, nestling myself between her legs and pushing them up and out of the way. "You mean to tell me you were sitting here all this time with nothing beneath those little shorts? That this pussy was just waiting for me?"

She nods, her lip between her teeth.

"Answer me, Sawyer," I demand.

"Yes," she says, her voice breathy as my finger slides up and down her slit slowly, urging her wetness to spread.

"No panties? Why not?" I say, letting the tip of my finger slip inside her, turning it in slow swipes as she writhes beneath me.

"Well," she breathes between moans, "if your idiot brother hadn't shown up, I was, oh...I was going to touch myself while thinking about you." I raise an eyebrow. *Fuck.*

"Oh yeah?" I ask softly. "You were gonna use this pretty hand," I say, lifting one of them and bringing it to my lips. I kiss the tips of her fingers then suck one into my mouth. "To touch this pretty little pussy," I say, leaning down to leave a gentle kiss right on her opening. She bucks her hips. "And think about me?"

She nods, pressing her head back into her pillow.

"Answer me," I demand again.

"Yes, and my, um...toy."

Oh, God.

"Toy?" I ask. She nods.

"Yes."

I slide my finger out of her, sucking on her arousal then pushing off the bed.

"Show me," I say. Her eyes widen.

"S-show you?" she says. I nod and take a step back, and she pushes up onto her elbows then scoots off the bed. Her eyes lock with mine, and she shimmies out of the shirt that's hanging off her shoulders. She puts her hands on me, guiding me backward toward the little armchair that sits by her window and shoving me down into it.

She turns around and walks to her nightstand, pulling the drawer open. She pulls out a small hot-pink object shaped like a small flower and walks toward me. She walks to the edge of the bed, only a few feet from where I sit in the chair, and lies back, spreading her legs wide so that I get the perfect view of the most beautiful and delicious pussy I've ever seen.

"Tell me what you do," I say, sitting back, wrapping a hand around my throbbing cock.

"I lie back, just like this," she says. "Then I warm myself up a tiny bit." She slides her hand down between her legs, letting her fingers play with her lips, spreading herself open and sliding in and out of her wetness. She uses her other hand to turn the toy on, then her eyes lock with mine again. "Then I start to think about you. About all the things you have done to me...or that I want you to do."

She puts the toy on her clit, moving it in slow circles as her eyes roll back in her head.

"What kinds of things?" I ask, pumping my hand on myself over my pants. But she sees me, and she stops, sitting up.

"No, sir," she says, motioning toward my hand on my crotch. "This is my time to shine. You just sit there and watch. No touching. Not even yourself."

I smirk, biting the inside of my lip before I obey, dropping myself and gripping onto either side of the chair. I don't know why I let her boss me around, but I do. It's fucking hot.

She smiles when I comply then lies back again.

JULIAN

"*I* picture you plowing into me, over and over," she moans, moving the toy up and down. "I usually think about you going down on me, the way you fuck me with your...oh, with your tongue," she breathes. *Fuck me. I'm about to combust.*

"What else?" I growl.

"I think about you throwing my legs over your shoulders while you put that huge cock into me, over and over and over..." she says, her voice trailing off as she moves the toy faster, the buzzing sound giving me convulsions. "Julian?" she whimpers.

"Yes, baby?"

"You gonna finish this, or should I?" she asks, and before she gets out the last syllable, I'm out of the chair, ripping my pants off. I snatch the toy out of her hand, throwing it across the room. She laughs.

"You better buy me a new one of those," she says as I grip her ankles, yanking her to the edge of the bed.

I look down at her glistening pussy, and I want to melt into it. I look up at her, our eyes locking as I spit on it. She moans, biting her lip again as I plunge into her. I know she's close, and God knows I am too. This doesn't need to be long, but it's going to be fucking amazing.

I hoist her legs up higher, lifting her ass up off the bed. The angle causes her to scream out immediately, clutching the blanket as she throws her head back.

"Christ, Julian," she sighs. "Oh, God."

I move my hips faster, my cock all up in her guts as I push her knees up and out, spreading her wide. I'm about to blow but only when she does. I lick the pad of my thumb then press it against her clit, matching my own rhythm inside of her.

"No need for that toy right now, princess," I growl. "You come for me. Now."

"Oh, Jesus," she cries out, digging her nails into my arms. "Fuck, Julian, I...oh, God, I think I'm, oh my god, I'm going to..."

I know what's happening. But I don't think she does.

I pull out of her, moving my hand as fast as it can go on her clit. And then it happens, in all its glory, spewing out of her like the sexiest fucking geyser I've ever seen. Her eyes are wide as she watches her own body, and I stand there happily, letting myself get soaked.

"Oh, my god!" she cries, bringing a hand to her face.

"That's my girl," I say, letting her get over the last little hump.

"I can't believe I...that's never happened," she says. "I'm sorry, I..."

I hold my hand up, the other wrapping around my cock that has its own heartbeat at this point.

"Don't you *ever* fucking apologize for anything this body does. Ever."

She nods.

"It's your turn," she says, slowing her breathing down and lying back. "And I want to see it."

My eyes widen.

"You want to see it?"

She nods, sliding her hand down to her navel.

"Right here," she says, pointing to her stomach. "I want to see what I do to you."

I growl, pushing her legs back up and plunging back inside, bringing myself closer to the edge again. She moans as the aftershocks crash through her, and when I know I'm close, I pull back out.

I grip myself, yanking the condom off and pumping fast until I blow all over her beautiful body. She smiles down like she's staring at the fruits of her labor.

"God, you're fucking sexy," she says. I laugh and shake my head as I catch my breath then pull her up slowly. I scoop her up, carrying her into the bathroom and turning on the shower. I wash her from head to toe, kissing her shoulders as I scrub her hair. She does the same when she washes mine, then we rinse off, get out, and get into her bed, staring out over the ocean.

She's curled on me, and I'm dragging lazy fingers up and down her arm as the moonlight brightens up the room.

"Julian?" she says sleepily, her eyes still closed.

"Yeah, baby?"

"I think I'm in love with you."

My heart stops beating in my chest for a moment.

The world stops spinning.

She doesn't look panicked. She doesn't seem nervous about the confession she just made. She doesn't look concerned that I might not return it.

She looks just as calm and at peace as she did a minute ago.

But *fuck*.

I *know* I'm in love with her.

I knew it early on, when nothing else mattered to me except for her safety.

I've never said it to anyone.

Not even my ex-fiancée.

We exchanged casual "I love yous" but nothing that held any true weight.

But now, I have this angel of a girl in this bed with me.

She doesn't want or need anything from me except for my time. If our lives never got more exciting than this little bed in this little room in this little apartment, it would be enough.

I would be enough.

I reach down and tilt her chin to me, and she slowly opens her sleepy emerald eyes.

"Sweet girl, I've been in love with you from the second time we met. I am going to give you anything and everything you could ever need," I whisper. She smiles, leaning forward to kiss my lips.

"Just stay right here, and your mission will be accomplished."

God, she really is perfect.

SAWYER

When I wake up, he's gone. And I quickly decide that I don't like that near as much as when he's wrapped around me. I hear him talking from the kitchen, and I reach over and grab his t-shirt from the night before and pull it on. I snort in his scent like I'm doing a line of coke and then make my way out.

He looks up at me and gives me that sexy-as-fuck half-smirk as he stirs the scrambled eggs in the sizzling pan in front of him. He's shirtless, by the way, and if I had any panties on, they'd already be damp from just the sight of him. Chestnut locks tousled from the night we had, his olive skin gleaming in the morning light that fills the space. I lean on the doorway and watch him, biting my lip. He puts a hand over the phone.

"You are gonna make me lose my damn mind coming out here like that. You better go put more clothes on unless you want me to fuck you again before breakfast," he whispers. Then he moves his hand. "What? Oh, did you hear that? Sorry, John. Yep, four-thirty tomorrow is fine. I'll be with my father, so we can take the call together. Yep. Alrighty. Bye-bye."

My lady boner deflates as quickly as it came on with the words "I'll be with my father," and I wait for him to explain.

"So, what'll it be? Eggs before sex, or sex before eggs?" he asks, flicking the stove off.

I laugh, walking around the island to him to give him a morning kiss. His hand slides up under the shirt as he takes a handful of my bare ass.

"You're seeing your dad tomorrow?" I ask. He smiles again, looking down at me.

"Yeah. We're meeting out at Bedell House tomorrow for my stepmom's birthday party. And, uh... I was kind of hoping you'd join me."

I swallow.

Whoa.

I feel my body get tense, and he must too. He puts the spatula down and wraps his other arm around me.

"No pressure, baby. I swear. It's fast, I know. If you want more time, that's completely—"

"I want to come," I cut him off. And I mean it. My heart might be racing, but I'm ready. The sexy half-smirk quickly grows into an all-out sexy grin, and he bends down to kiss me again, squeezing me tight.

"Are you sure? I'm really not trying to pressure

you..." he starts, but I step up onto my tiptoes and kiss him again.

"I want to do this," I tell him between kisses. Then I jump up and wrap my legs around his waist. "And to answer your earlier question, sex before eggs."

He smiles, carrying me back toward the bedroom, but stops and lays me down on the table.

We don't even make it to my room.

* * *

AFTER ANOTHER ROUND on my dining table—well, I guess *his* table—and one more in the shower, we're dressed and clothed.

"Pack for a few nights," he tells me as he kisses me and walks out of my bedroom to take a call. A few? How many is a few? Christmas is at the end of this week, and to be honest, I'm fucking dreading it. I've never spent Christmas without my mom, and Julian and I literally just decided yesterday that we were a couple, so asking about holidays together feels a little quick. That, and he's the third richest man in the world. He might have a plan or two already.

I throw enough clothes in my bag for four days, which leads me to Christmas Eve. He can bring up the holiday if he wants to spend it together, but as the much younger, much poorer member of this couple, it won't be me.

There's just one issue, though, and I rush back out of my room. I walk back out to him just as he's hanging up his call, and he turns to me and smiles, eyebrows drawing together as soon as he sees the look on my face.

"What is it, baby?"

"I have nothing to wear to meet your dad. What do I wear? I have one dress, and I don't know if it's...*fuck,*" I say, storming back into my room and flinging my closet back open. I hear him chuckle behind me as he makes his way to me, grabbing my waist and spinning me around to face him.

"We're going shopping in the city before we go to Bedell House tomorrow," he tells me. "You can pick a few things out, and then we'll stay at my apartment tonight and head there in the morning. Stop panicking." He kisses me, and I feel myself let out a sigh of relief. But him spending money on me still feels weird. I know that, technically, he's made more money before he even slides his credit card any time he purchases anything. But it doesn't make me feel less bad about it.

He reaches up and tugs on my chin, releasing my lip from my teeth.

"If you don't stop biting this lip, I will," he says. Then he leans forward, pulling me closer to him. "Stop worrying about the money, Sawyer. Let me spoil you while I still can."

I pull back, raising an eyebrow.

"What does that mean?" I ask. He breathes in deep, the expression on his face getting a little more serious, like he is a little wary of telling me more. Instead, he reaches out a hand to me.

"I'll tell you more in the car," he says. "Tyler's here."

I TRY to bring it up again multiple times throughout the day, but it's hard between a gourmet picnic lunch in Central Park, shopping on Fifth Avenue, and dinner at Delmonico's. I got my first ever pair of designer shoes that I'm pretty positive I'll end up breaking my ankles in. I got an evening dress for the party, another more casual dress for dinner, and a few new blouses. He tried to get me into another few stores, but I refused.

"I think this is the least amount I've..." His voice trails off as he opens the door to the Escalade, and we both freeze. I swallow.

"The least you've spent on a woman?" I ask.

"I'm sorry," he says. I don't say anything, just climb in. The ride through the city to his apartment is awkwardly quiet. He reaches for my hand, and I let him take it but keep my eyes out the window. I'm not sure what to make of his accidental comment.

I'm quiet until we get into the apartment, and Tyler leaves us to it. I walk inside, putting my purse down on the entryway table. Before I can make it farther into the penthouse, I feel his big hands on me, spinning me back into him.

"Hey," he says, wrapping his body around mine. "Look at me, Sawyer. Please." I swallow the lump in my throat. I'm confused. I don't even know what's upsetting me. It's not like I didn't know he's been with other women. But thinking about it isn't really all that fun. "Hey," he whispers, tilting my head up to look at him. Finally, I do. "I'm sorry. That was a dumb thing for me to say."

"It's okay," I say with a shrug and a very forced smile. But he shakes his head.

"It's not," he says. My eyes drop, but he gently grabs my chin again, forcing my eyes back. "I didn't mean anything by it. I just...I want you to understand how special you are to me, Sawyer. And I get that bringing up other women probably wasn't exactly the smartest way to do that."

I chuckle and shake my head, but his expression stays sincere.

"I've never been with someone who...who didn't need anything from me. Who wasn't in a rush to have our pictures all over the internet together. Who took their time with me like you have. I have the whole fucking world at my fingertips, but I never had a safe place to land...until you. All I meant tonight was that it was...it was like pulling teeth to get you to let me buy you anything, rather than you taking advantage of it or expecting it—which, ironically, just makes me want to spoil you more. But I'm sorry. I didn't mean to compare, because the truth is, there is no comparison to you, Sawyer."

I don't even realize that my eyes are filled with tears until he reaches his thumbs up to swipe them away. It's a funny coincidence, because he is also my safe place to land. He's air when I can't take a deep breath. He's a solution when, before, I only had problems. He gives my mind a break and has a way of taking command when my brain is fried from too much life. And it breaks me that he's never felt like that for someone. But I'm so glad that it gets to be me.

"Julian, you are so much more than your money or your last name," I whisper. "I'm sorry no one has ever showed you that. But I'm going to."

I swallow back another lump when I realize that his eyes are getting glassy. He smiles down at me, his thumbs stroking my cheeks.

He bends down and picks me up, carrying me like a child up to his suite. His tongue is in my mouth the whole way, and mine is returning the favor. He sets me down on the heated tiles of his massive bathroom and turns the water on in the gigantic soaking tub that sits at the back of the room next to the wall of floor-to-ceiling windows. The Empire State Building is lit up for Christmas, and the city looks breathtaking. He tests out the water temperature then walks back to me, unzipping my jeans and pulling my shirt up over my head. He unhooks my bra and pulls down my panties then picks me back up and carries me to the tub, setting me gently in the warm water. He dumps in some bubbles and some bath salts then takes off his own clothes and sinks in with me. We face each other, our heads resting on either edge, and I let myself draw in a deep breath.

"This isn't right," he says, then he leans forward,

grabs my arm, and pulls me to him, spinning me around so that my back is to his chest. I giggle as we nestle back into the water, and I can't remember a time in my life when I have ever felt this at ease. We lie in silence for a little bit, touching, rubbing, exploring. And while I know the night will inevitably end with him inside me, this moment feels beyond sexual. It's sensual and intimate. Like our bodies are getting to know each other in another way.

But alas, I'm nosey as fuck.

And I've waited long enough to bring it up again.

"Julian?"

"Hmm?"

"What did you mean earlier, when you said 'let me spoil you while I still can'?"

I feel his chest vibrate underneath me as a chuckle rolls out of him.

"I was wondering when this would come up again," he says. I sit up, turning to look at him. I sit on top of him so I'm facing him, scooting closer so that my pussy is on top of his cock. I roll forward slightly, and I see his eyebrow raise.

"I'm serious," I say.

A devious smile tugs at his lips.

"I'm sorry," he laughs, "but do you expect me to have a serious conversation with you while you're literally sitting on my cock?"

I roll forward and backward again, letting myself drag up and down his shaft.

"If you tell me, I'll move a little farther south," I

say. My breasts bob between us, bubbles splayed around them.

His hands slide around my hips, cupping my ass, and he blows out a long breath.

"Alright, alright," he says. "Let's dry off. I can't concentrate like this."

In a few moments time, we're dried off, naked, and in his bed.

"Okay," he says as he pulls me into him, "well, I know you've done your homework. You've read about my father. And most of what you've read is probably true. The discrimination lawsuits, unlawful layoffs, all of it."

I swallow.

Yikes. I was afraid of that.

SAWYER

"*E*verett Enterprises has never been as lucrative as it's been under his reign," he goes on. "It's never had more acquisitions; it's never expanded at this rate. My father launched us further ahead than my great-grandfather ever could have imagined. But the thing is, it's also further ahead than we ever needed to be, and we've left too many people behind."

I roll over to him, tucking my hands under my head, hanging on every word he says.

"My grandfather, he was...God, he was everything I want to be in a man. He knew that our money could change things. He knew that any other man could have struck oil the way his dad had. That it easily could have been some other lucky bastard. He thought that if we were going to take from the land, we should give back too. He used to give away thousands and thousands of acres to different communities for them to build on. He'd hand-pick a few hundred small businesses every year to fund. Not to invest in; he'd never take a return. Just to get them started. On Christmas every year, he'd take us into the city and let my brothers and me each pick a different apartment building. And then we'd walk around to every single door and give each family a thousand dollars. My dad never came."

His eyes look heavy now.

"Old money is different than the type of money we have now. It grew slower. It was harder to come by. And my grandfather thought that he was given the opportunities that he was because others couldn't. He believed in philanthropy. By the time he died, he had almost lost his billionaire status because he'd given so much away. And that's what we're going to do."

My eyes grow wide. *We?*

"Who's we?" I ask him.

"My brothers and me—well, at least me and Keaton. My dad...he has to think he's in charge. There is a specific way you have to work him. Keaton, he can't stand it. He donated his entire trust fund to different charities. He has put a ton of his own money into a few non-profits he started and lives well beneath his means. That's his way of combating it. But me, I'm working my dad in a different way. I'm learning the ins and outs of the businesses. I'm learning the key players. I'm making small moves when I can. And eventually, I'll be CEO. And when that day comes, we have a plan in place to spread the money out so much that we will lose that same status. But it has to be done carefully so that all of this money and power doesn't fall back into the hands of another greed-stricken man who will just keep building the empire the way my dad has. Instead, we're going to break it off, piece by piece, essentially giving away small portions of our businesses to small business owners.

We will have contracts in place that will ensure diversity, equal pay, all that kind of stuff, so that no one ever gets screwed over by Everett Enterprises ever again. And Keaton and I will remain members of the board who will oversee it all so we can make sure of it."

God, I really didn't think he could be any sexier... until right now.

"What about Brooks?" I ask.

"Brooks...he's used to this lifestyle. My granddad died when he was young. He's never known that side of our family legacy. But I know we can get him there. He's not against it, but he's not really for it either. He's not really for anything, except blondes, booze, and a good time."

I nod.

"Julian?"

"Yeah, baby?"

"That's the most amazing thing," I tell him. "And you're so fucking hot." He laughs, and I push him onto his back. And without thinking, I grind myself against him a few times then take him inside of me. And then my eyes widen. He doesn't have a condom on. Oh, God, it feels good. I want him like this, no barrier, so close. But I don't want to freak him out. I don't want him thinking I'm trying to get knocked up to hold onto anything.

"I'm sorry," I say, frozen on top of him. "I...I wasn't thinking. I'm not on the pill and..." I go to move, but he grips my hips.

"Sawyer," he says, "I had a vasectomy. It's totally your call. I get tested after every partner. And the only person I've been with in the last six months is you."

Whoa. That's a lot to take in.

But so is his giant cock. And knowing I can ride it to my heart's desire right now? Yeah, the overthinking about all the information he just laid on me will have to come at a different time.

I move my hips slow at first, feeling every inch of him touching every inch of me.

"Oh, God," I moan. I suck my teeth as I move, letting him hit the deepest parts of me.

"That's my girl," he says. "Bounce for me, baby. Let me see what you can do."

Fuck, the praise.

I reach out, taking his hands and putting them on my breasts. He squeezes and massages them, tugging at my nipples until they peak. I want to do dirty things to him, and I want him to do them back. But this night feels bigger than dirty sex. And I think he feels it too. He hooks his hands under my knees and flips me onto my back before plunging back into me. He cages my head between his arms, staring down at me while he thrusts in and out of me.

"Sawyer," he whispers, "you're everything."

Then he reaches his hand down between us, circling my clit as he pounds into me. We come moments apart from each other, collapsing into a twisted ball of sweat and sex and soul-crushing adoration.

JULIAN

*S*he makes even the craziest of days feel calmer. I've put out three different fires from my phone this morning all while she's curled up, snoring on my other arm. I love when she snores. She doesn't do it all the time, but I like to watch her while she does it. I love how deep of a sleep she's in. How her whole body is relaxed. She knows, even in her sleep, that she's as safe as she could be.

What I wouldn't give to stay like this. To keep her all to myself. To show her things she's never seen before. To take care of all her worries. For her to never know fear again. I met her in fear. And I want to be the one to take it all away.

But in just a few hours, the real test will take place. Not of whether or not my family likes her; I truly couldn't care less what they think of her. In fact, in some ways, it would be easier if they didn't like her. It would give me a reason to keep her away. But it'll be the test of whether or not she really wants this life.

A few minutes later, she bats her long lashes a few times and stretches, and I lean over to kiss her as the blinds lift, letting the sunlight and city in.

"Good morning, pretty girl," I whisper. She smiles against my lips, wrapping her arms around my neck and nestling into me.

"Good morning," she says. She rubs her eyes and blinks a few times. "Do you not want kids?"

I choke out a surprised laughed. She forgets nothing and wastes almost no time getting the answers she's looking for.

"I was wondering how long it would take before that came up, but I guess I have my answer."

She shrugs.

"You knew I wouldn't just let that go," she says. I chuckle again as I kiss her forehead.

"Yes, I sure did," I say. "I'd love to have kids one day."

"But you're all sewn up," she says.

"It's reversible," I say. "I did it for protection more than anything else. Both for me, but also for my future children. I made a promise to myself at a young age that I'd never put a kid through what my brothers and I went through. I had to be absolutely sure that it was the right person I was making them with. That I could show them what love is."

She just stares at me, wide-eyed. Then she nods, seemingly satisfied with that response.

"Are you ready for today?" I whisper against her. She nods.

"I was born ready, baby," she says. I smile. And I know she's right. I'm pretty sure there's nothing she can't handle.

A FEW HOURS LATER, we're packed and in the Escalade, and Russ is headed in the direction of Bedell House. She's still, but I can feel her nervous energy radiating through the car. I reach over and put my hand on hers, holding onto it tight—the same way I did that very first day she got into this car. I didn't know her then. Or at least, I thought I didn't. Some part of me did, though. Some part of me knew that I needed to get her out. I needed to save her the way she saved me. And now I know why. Because there is no life without her.

She looks down at our interlocked fingers, and a faint smile creeps onto her lips as she turns to me. There they are. Those big green eyes that suck me in and turn me into a complete puddle. I lift her hand to my lips and press a soft kiss to her knuckles. I don't have to say anything. She knows what I'm thinking.

That it's all going to be okay. That I'm right here.

A LITTLE WHILE LATER, we're pulling up to the gate, Russ is scanning his hand, and we're pulling up the mile-long driveway onto the property. Russ pulls around to the front door, and the doormen greet us, shaking hands with Russ and grabbing all of our stuff from the back.

"Just to your suite, Mr. Julian?" an old man with wispy white hair asks. I clap his back.

"That would be great. Thank you, Thomas," I say. "Always great to see you." Thomas smiles and nods as he walks off with our things, another one of the younger doormen in tow. "Thomas has worked here on the property since my grandfather owned it. They met as kids. His father worked here before him, and my great-grandfather would let him bring his son to work so the boys could play. He never married, and though we tried to get him to retire, he refuses. My grandfather left him a significant amount of money in his will when he passed, but Thomas says working here keeps him young. So the younger guys try to lighten the load for him when he lets them," I explain.

She smiles.

"That's really cool," she says. Just as we're walking up the front steps, Angelina's shrill voice shrieks my name as she clicks across the foyer and out onto the main landing toward us. She holds her hands up to my face, pulling me in and kissing my cheeks.

"Hey, Angelina," I say, giving her a very low-effort hug back. "It's good to see you again. Happy birthday." She smiles up at me, slowly turning to Sawyer with surprise painted all over her perfectly made-up face.

Sawyer and I decided not to give anyone else in the family a heads-up. I had told her that the less people we told in advance, the better. It would give everyone less time to dig, pry, and focus on her. Plus, with the party tonight, there will be even less time for us to be the center of conversation.

"And who do we have here?" Angelina asks, trying like hell to keep her voice as light and airy as possible. I pull Sawyer into me, wrapping my arm around her waist.

"This is Sawyer," I tell her. I freeze for a moment as all three of us wait to see if there is more to the intro-duction. A label. But none feel right. *Girlfriend* feels too shallow, like it doesn't cover enough, so I turn back to Angelina. "She's with me," I say simply. "Sawyer, this is my father's wife, Angelina."

Sawyer sticks out a hand, and Angelina takes it, the fakest of smiles spreading across her lips. She puts a manicured hand to her chest.

"I didn't realize you were bringing a date," Angelina says, her eyes flashing back to me for a moment then back to Sawyer. "It's very nice to meet you, Sawyer."

But I want to be clear.

"Oh, she's not just a date," I say, my grip on her tightening. "We're dating. We're together."

JULIAN

*A*ngelina's eyes widen, her head nodding slowly. For the years she's been around, I've never brought a woman to any event, let alone announced that I was seeing someone. But seeing the look in her eyes, I know she's also wondering how much of the spotlight will be taken off her this week because of it. If I can help it, it'll be all about Angelina. I'll protect Sawyer as long as I possibly can.

"Thank you," Sawyer says, "it's so nice to meet you too." We stand in silence for a moment before Angelina waves us in, as if it's her name on the deed to this place and not mine or my brothers'. But I let her go. We follow her inside, and the staff is finishing up final touches on decorations around the house. I feel Sawyer's grip on my hand tighten as she takes it all in again, this time a little less rushed and a little less hushed.

My father—or, presumably, Angelina under the

guise of my father—has really outdone himself for this. There are tables set up all over the main halls, decorations on what feels like every inch of the house, and a large portrait of Angelina hanging in the center of the foyer that he apparently had commissioned.

I can see the stage being set up in the main hall to my right, and I can hear the AV guys testing the sound system. I look down at Sawyer, and she looks back up at me.

"I can't believe this is your house," she breathes out with a giggle. I smile.

"It's not," I remind her. "None of us live here full time. It's more of a venue."

"Finally!" I hear Brooks say as he walks down the right side of the main staircase. He makes his way to us, bending down to hug Sawyer first then me.

"You positive about this, Big Brother? It's gonna be a fiasco," he whispers in my ear. I just smile and pat his back. There's no turning back now.

"Well, what do we have here?" I hear my father's booming voice call from the top of the stairs, looking down at us like he's a god. Our eyes meet, and I hate how much I look like him. I love my father, but I know there is something evil in him. And I worry every day that if I don't do enough, that evil will come out in me too.

He walks down the stairs like he's floating, his thick gold ring that belonged to my grandfather gleaming under the chandeliers. When he makes it to the floor, he looks at us. Angelina appears at his side, just as she always does, but his eyes are on me and then on Sawyer.

"Julian has brought, uh…" Angelina's voice starts to trail off.

"Hey, Dad," I say as we stand feet apart now. "This is Sawyer."

His eyes stay locked with mine for a moment longer, like he's trying to figure something out. Then he looks to Sawyer.

"Miss Sawyer," he says, holding his hand out. She puts hers in it, but rather than shaking it, he turns it and kisses it. She clears her throat quietly.

"Hi, Mr. Everett. It's—"

"Cato, please," he corrects her, looking back and forth between her and me. "Will you be joining us for Angelina's party?"

"Yes, she will," I interject. "Sawyer and I have been dating for a few weeks. I wanted to introduce her to the family."

My dad's head tilts back slowly, a half-smile on his lips.

"Well, how 'bout that," he says. "I've never known my son to bring a date to an event, let alone a whole girlfriend. You must be special, Sawyer."

It sounds nice enough, but I can feel the underlying intent.

What do you want from this?
How old are you?

"Thank you," she says, "but I think Julian is pretty special."

189

"Yes," my father says. "Many do, my dear." *Fucker.* Our eyes lock, and I glare at him. Within sixty seconds of meeting her, he's already pointing out that she's after the money. But I won't back down.

"I'm sure many think that his name and his fortune are special," she says, and I snap my mouth shut. "But I don't know that many others know how much of what makes him so incredible goes so far beyond that. Or that he'd be just as amazing without all of this," she says, waving her hand.

Damn.

Brooks's eyes are wide, and a surprised smile creeps onto his lips.

I wait for a moment to gauge my father's reaction, but slowly, he smiles too.

"Indeed," he says. "Only those closest to him know all that he has to offer." Sawyer nods, never taking her eyes from his. "Well, we have a few hours until the party. Lunch will be served on the main terrace in about twenty minutes for the family. See you all in a bit, yes?"

I nod, taking Sawyer's hand as my father and Angelina walk past us, an event planner accosting them as they make their way out of the room.

"Damn!" Brooks says. "That was slick, Sawyer. Way to not let the man get ya down." He pats our backs as he walks through the halls. She turns to me slowly, her bottom lip between her teeth.

"I'm sorry," she says. "I just...I could feel him..."

I lean down to kiss her.

"Do you realize you just took on the richest man on the planet? You're kind of a badass, Sawyer Willis."

She smiles as I pull away from her, taking her hand and leading her through the halls to the family wing. After a few minutes of walking, retina scanning, and sneaking kisses in hidden stairwells, we are in the family wing and in my suite. Thomas and the guys have already brought all of our things, and a fire is already roaring in the fireplace. She looks around, trailing her fingers across the furniture and the edge of the bed until she makes her way to the huge windows that look out over the water.

"God, this is beautiful," she says. I wrap my arms around her, nuzzling into her neck and hair.

"And I'd give it all up in a heartbeat for you," I say. She spins to me slowly, pressing up on her tiptoes to kiss me.

"You can chill with all of that," she says. "You're gonna get laid tonight, okay, Everett?" Her lips pull up into a half-smile, and I laugh as I nuzzle her again, scooping her up and carrying her to the bed where I almost lost myself with her before.

"Tonight? Who agreed to wait till tonight?" I say as I cover her neck and chest with soft kisses. She squirms beneath me, laughing and running her hands over my ass.

"I did," she says, finally pushing me off playfully. "I have brunch with the billionaires. I gotta be on my A-game and not freshly fucked."

I laugh as she shakes her ass, walking toward her luggage.

"I'll give you a pass," I tell her. "But you will be walking around this place 'freshly fucked' a whole fucking lot this week."

She bites her lip and smiles as she looks at me.

"Promise?"

SAWYER

I change into one of the more casual dresses that Julian bought me, put on some boots, and fluff my hair a bit before I make my way back out of the bathroom. He's looking just as panty-soaking hot as always, and what I wouldn't give to let him take me right here, right now. But instead, I've got a table full of the world's richest people to piss off tonight.

We decide to take the outdoor route, and I bask in the chilly fall air as he leads me around the house to the back terrace. There's a big, long table set up with a whole friggin' feast and servers everywhere. Cato and Angelina sit at one end of the table, Brooks on one side, and two empty seats on the other for us.

"Hope you're hungry," Angelina says, clapping her hands together. "I've had Emile get some fresh salmon from the seafood market."

My mouth waters.

I do love a good piece of salmon.

"No Keaton?" Julian asks as he pulls my chair out for me. Cato flashes him a look and another one of those sly smiles he seems to be full of.

"He won't be making it out for the party," Cato says. "But I'm sure you already knew that, eh, son?"

Julian doesn't respond, just sits down next to me.

The servers bring us drinks, appetizers, and salads all before the main course comes out, and I wonder how they're not all four hundred pounds. I'm stuffed before I even finish my salad.

Julian reaches for my hand under the table, and at first, I think it's meant to be that way. But then, he leans back in his chair, holding it out in the open for the world to see. Cato glances at us then sits back in his own chair while the pre-courses are cleared from the table.

"So," he says, "Sawyer. Tell us how you met our Julian."

I swallow. I look at him, but he just smiles, nodding.

We don't need to hide anything.

"I, uh...I'm actually a student at Carrington," I say. Cato's eyes flash to Julian then back to me. "I was trying to escape campus the day of the shooting, and—"

"She saved my life that day," Julian says, looking nowhere but at me. His father's eyes grow wide as they land on me. "I was just arriving to campus for my speech when the shooter had started. Sawyer was running and saw us. She stopped us from walking right in the shooter's direction. We ended up helping her get off campus, and we've been attached ever since."

The table is silent, and I feel my palm getting clammy pressed up against Julian's. But he doesn't budge. In fact, he just squeezes it tighter, stroking the back of my hand with his thumb.

"Well, I, uh...I don't know what to say, Sawyer," Cato says, his eyes moving back and forth between me and Julian. "And I'm not a man who is rendered speechless often. Thank you. Thank you for warning my son."

I look up at him, our eyes locked. I know there are a lot of complicated sides to this man, but the look in his eyes right now feels genuine. And I'm uncomfortable. I don't like to be thanked. I don't like to be complimented. And I do not know what to do with this.

Deflect. Deflect.

"I was just in the right place at the right time," I reiterate. "Julian is the one who got me out."

"Sounds like you saved each other," Brooks chimes in, presumably before Cato can jump back on the obviously-you're-just-using-my-son train. I look at him, and he smiles softly.

"That's what we like to think," Julian says, looking down at me and kissing the top of my head.

"So you're a college student, then," Cato says, a statement rather than a question. I nod. "Makes you seem like an old man, Julian," he says with a coy smile.

"Just taking notes from you, Dad," Julian quips

with a nod in Angelina's direction. Cato smiles and clears his throat, turning back to me.

"And what is it you're studying?"

"Communications," I say. "My track is PR, but I'm not sure what I want to do yet. Just something to pay the bills and help my mom out."

I figure there's no use in playing any games or pretending to have decorum that I most certainly don't. Lay it all out for them so there is nothing left for them to sniff out. Besides, I lead a pretty boring, lower-middle-class life. Sniff away.

"And where are you from?"

"Seattle," I say. "Actually, I'm going back in a few days to see my mom for the holidays. It'll be a fast turnaround, but I can't wait to see her just for a little while."

Cato smiles, hanging on every word I say.

"Is it just you and your mom, then?" Angelina asks, taking a sip of her wine. I nod.

"Yep, just us," I say.

"And why the fast turnaround? Doesn't the university get a few weeks off for the semester break?" Cato asks.

"Yes, we do. Classes have been canceled since the shooting, anyway. But I can't take too many days off work." This catches him by surprise.

"Ah, I see. And what do you do for work?"

"I work as a clerk at a mini-mart off campus," I say. "Nothing fancy, but it pays for what my scholarships don't."

"Scholarships, plural," Cato says. "Impressive. Sounds like you're no stranger to hard work, Sawyer."

I shake my head.

"Doesn't scare me," I say.

He doesn't say much else, but throughout the rest of lunch, I can feel his eyes on us, watching the way we interact, catching any display of affection Julian may have toward me. But every time he looks at us, I look back. I lock my eyes on him.

"Alright," Angelina finally says, clapping her hands together, "it's about that time. The stylists should be here any minute. Sawyer, why don't you come with me? We can get pampered before the party."

I swallow, looking at Julian, who looks more uneasy than I am. But I turn back to Angelina and smile.

"That sounds like fun," I tell her. "Anything for the birthday girl."

She smiles and stands up from the table while all three of the men follow suit.

"You good?" Julian asks me. I smile and nod, trying to look way more comfortable than I already am.

"Yeah, it's girl time," I say with a wink. He smiles.

"We will be in my father's study on a call," he says. "Text or call me if you need me."

I nod, then Angelina holds a hand out in my direction, and I take it, following her off the terrace and into the maze that is Bedell House.

I follow her blindly through the halls until I figure

out that we're back in the family wing again—only, on the other side of it.

"Have you been here before?" she asks as she leads me to the last door of the hall. I nod.

"Just once, briefly. Not that that would help much," I chuckle. "This place is insane." She smiles as she opens the door, leading me into yet another giant suite.

"It is," she says. "And so beautiful. And deserving of so much love, but it hardly gets any anymore."

I follow her through the room into what can only be described as the biggest fucking closet on the fucking planet. She hits a light switch, and a salon chair moves out from the back of the room to the center of it. The lights change from dim overheads to brighter fluorescents, and Beyonce begins to play over the surround sound. The walls are lined with floor-length gowns, shoes, and bags, and huge diamond jewelry sits on every corner encased in thick glass.

"This feels fake," I say. Angelina laughs as she kicks her shoes off on the floor and walks through the room into the bathroom.

"It does," she says. "A lot of this isn't mine," she calls from the bathroom. "Most of it was actually Catherine's, Cato's mother." She comes back out wrapped in a silk robe and takes a seat in the salon chair. She motions to a chaise in the corner of the room. "Please, sit." A moment later, one of the staff brings in a tray of mimosas, and Angelina looks at me. "Just something to take the edge off."

We hold our glasses up in the air, then she sits back in the chair as we sip in awkward silence.

"I still can't believe this is real," I murmur as I look around. Angelina sighs.

"I know," she says. "I'll never be used to it. And I know it's fleeting, so I try to soak in every moment."

My eyes drop to hers.

"Fleeting?" I ask. She tilts her flute up, emptying it into her mouth.

"Of course, hon," she says. "Men like the Everetts... they can have everything and anything they want. Literally. No exaggeration. Businesses, homes, entire towns if they wanted. There is no limit. And you and me? We're just stops on the way, sweetie. I know it. I know that, right now, I have enough of what Cato wants to keep him. But my day will come. I can feel it starting. The solo business trips. The meetings all day, the calls all night. But when he's gone, I get to be here, or in one of our other homes, playing queen of the castle. I know Cato's life will go on long after me. So now, I spend my time planning how mine will go after him."

I swallow.

We're just stops on the way.

I think she can feel the tension she's created, so she clears her throat as she stands up to grab another robe from a hanger.

"Enough of that," she says. "It's my birthday, and we're going to celebrate. Go put this on."

JULIAN

"How much longer do I give them before I go busting in there to save her?" I ask rhetorically.

"She's *fine,* dude," Brooks says behind me, flipping through the channels on the television in the rec room. "Let her get her pamper on."

I sigh, rubbing my temples as I fall into the couch.

I stare out over the garden, wishing like hell I could sneak off with her and get lost.

"You know Dad is super suspicious, right?" Brooks goes on, never taking his eyes off the TV.

"No shit," I say.

"I'm sure he thinks she's after—"

"I don't give a damn, Brooks," I say. "He'd be one to talk if he was concerned a woman was after my money while planning a million-dollar party for his third wife."

Brooks smiles and shrugs.

"Not saying you're wrong, Big Brother," he says, "but he's the king."

Like he heard us, Cato enters the room, dressed to the nines in a suit that makes him look as suave as ever.

"Are we ready, boys?" he asks. Brooks whistles, popping up.

"Damn, Pops," he says, "looking sharp as always."

"I try," he says with a modest shoulder pop. "No sign of the ladies yet, eh?"

I shake my head as we make our way toward him.

"Not yet," I say.

"Ah, let her have her fun," he says. "I trust you've taken care of—"

"Dad, the reason it took this long for me to tell you about her was because *she* didn't know if she wanted it out. You don't need to worry. But I just want to confirm again that there is not supposed to be any press here. I promised her."

My father nods slowly.

"No press," he says, his eyebrows knit together like he's not quite sure what to think about someone who *doesn't* want press.

Trust me, Pops. Been there.

"Come," he says, leading us out the door of the family wing and into the main living area. Just as we're walking out, so are the stylists from Angelina's suite. Her assistant, Diana, scurries out with a headset in.

"Yep. Great. Open doors in five," she says into it

then turns to us with a smile. "Evening, sir. Miss Angelina is all ready. Now, her intro will be at eight on the dot. Gives guests about thirty minutes to arrive. We will do hors d'oeuvres in the foyer hall, bars will be open, and then we will call everyone into the main hall for her introduction."

As she's giving her instructions, though, the door to the suite opens again, and my beautiful girl steps out. She's wearing the gown I bought her, a deep navy that hugs her body in all the right places, with heels that I want to take off and chuck across the room.

She looks like a fucking goddess, and it's all I can do not to rip it off her right now.

"Jesus," I cough out as I walk toward her. She bites her lip, and I bend down to kiss her, careful not to smudge anything. "You look...unreal."

"Yes, breathtaking, Sawyer," my father chimes in as he walks past us toward the main house.

"Fuckin' smoke show is what you are, girl," Brooks says, and I whip my head to him.

"I'll kill you where you stand," I warn him. "Go."

They both laugh as he walks by us, and then I hold her at arm's length.

"Let me get a good look," I say. "My god, woman. You're liable to kill me." She laughs, then I see her hand reach for her neck, and my heart stops for a moment. She's got on the diamond-and-sapphire necklace that my grandfather gave my grandmother when they moved back to Bedell House. The story was that the Duchess of Edinburgh gave it as a gift herself, although we never confirmed it. When he bought it for her, she wore it every single day until she died. My grandfather wanted to bury her with it, but my father convinced him not to. And I know for a fact that he has it appraised every year, despite the fact that it's willed to me when he dies.

It's the only material thing that has ever meant anything to me, because it reminds me of the two people who showed me what a real love looked like.

And now it's on her neck.

"Angelina told me I should wear it," she says. "She said it matched the dress so well. But I don't know, I...I feel...I think I should put it back. It's not—"

I stop her, reaching for her hands and bringing them down from her neck.

"Wear it," I whisper as I step closer to her. "Please. Please keep it on."

Her eyes scan mine for more of an explanation, but I don't give one, and bless her soul, she doesn't ask. I kiss her one more time before I take her hand, just as Connie rushes us out the wing and toward the main house.

For the most part, the night goes off without a hitch. A few of my relatives are here, but it's mostly filled with Angelina's "friends," my father's many, many business associates, and a few celebrities. While most people would gawk, Sawyer just takes it all in stride, not stumbling once on any introduction. I catch the eyes on us all night, but no one asks, and luckily enough, there is a strict agenda, complete with a video montage, a live band playing a song for Angelina and my father to dance to, and a call-in video chat with the Prince of Norway, wishing her a happy birthday.

Just as the cake is being cut, I pull Sawyer to the back of the banquet hall at a cocktail table. She's sipping on the same glass of wine I got her an hour ago, and I'm finishing off my last beer of the evening.

I'm about to suggest that we sneak away when I hear his booming voice.

Fuck.

"And how are we faring tonight, Sawyer?" my father asks as he approaches us, flanked by four or five men who have been working for our family since my grandfather took over. Men who my family has made richer than Midas over the years. Men who have sold their souls to the devil.

"Faring just fine, Cato, thank you," she says, holding her glass up. "This has been an amazing party."

He laughs heartily as he puts his glass down on our table.

"This here is Sawyer, boys," he says with a head nod in her direction. "Julian surprised us with her just today. They've apparently been dating."

There are some "hmms" and "ahhs" coming from the men around us, and I instinctively move closer to her. I keep my eye on him, trying to figure out what angle he's going for.

"She's a student," Cato goes on, and I see his eyes narrow in on her, locked in an accusatory gaze. "Like father, like son, eh, boys?" He looks around at them, and they all bust into a fit of fake laughter. "So what does that make you, Sawyer? Twenty-one, twenty-two?"

"Twenty-two," she says, her eyes narrowed back on him.

"So much life yet still to live," he says, his voice growing a little more serious. "And to think, your *boyfriend* here...he's lived quite a life. We all have. And you're just starting out. Probably not even sure what you really want out of life. Julian here, though...I'm sure he could help with that. When you're a struggling college student, a billionaire boyfriend is probably nice to have, eh?"

God dammit, Cato.

The men chuckle behind him, but he doesn't laugh. He just stays locked on her as I start to see red.

"Cato—" I start, but she puts her hand to my chest, stopping me. She keeps the same smile on her face as she sets her glass down.

"It's so interesting, though, when you really think about it. Here I am, what, forty, fifty years younger than you, Cato? I have no 'wealth.' I own nothing. No property, no assets. And yet, I have still lived so many experiences in my simple, short little life that you never have, nor ever will."

I look at her, fighting a smile. Then my eyes find my father's. I want to tackle him to the ground in front of all his friends. But my girl doesn't need me to.

"Oh?" he says, his voice getting a bit more stiff as

he sets his glass down. "And what, pray tell, experience do you have that you think I so desperately need, my dear?" he asks, condescension dripping from his lips. But that perfect little smile just stays on her lips.

"Well, for starters, have you ever worked for someone other than your father, Cato? Or yourself? Has a company that wasn't owned by your family's estate ever employed you? Have you ever relied on grants, scholarships, multiple jobs to pay the bills? Have you ever *paid* a bill, or do you have someone who does that for you?" She pauses for a moment, and an awkward but beautiful silence shrouds us. She chuckles to herself. "Imagine that. Poor, simple, broke college student from Seattle...more worldly than the richest man on the planet. Excuse me."

She turns on her heel and rushes past us, and I turn to my father.

"You tried, just like we all knew you would. But you won't mess this up for me, Dad. And you can't beat her with your little mind games. Careful, your insecurity is showing."

And then I follow her out of the room. I see the train of her gown dragging around the corridor, and I jog to catch up. She's running toward the side door, but I catch her just in time. I spin her around, but she won't look up at me. I cup her face and tilt her eyes up to mine.

"I'm sorry," she says. "I shouldn't have—"

"I love you," I say. Her eyes widen, tears still

pricking the corners. Her lips part as she stares up at me. "Can I take you somewhere?"

She nods slowly.

"Shouldn't we...shouldn't I probably leave?"

I laugh.

"Oh, we're leaving the party. Just not leaving the property."

I lead her down the south hallway to the old servants' door that leads to the side of the garden. When we get outside, she pauses to take off her shoes. I bend down in front of her, and she stares at me.

"What are you doing?"

"I'm not having you walk a half-mile barefoot. Get on," I say. She laughs.

"There is no way I'm—"

I don't give her another minute to argue. I throw her over my shoulder instead, walking through the garden as she giggles behind me.

"Julian! What if someone sees? You're supposed to be all important and serious," she says. I laugh.

"I know. Imagine my father's surprise when he has to explain this," I say, laughing as I make it around through the other end of the garden. We get to the eastern side of the house, and I set her down. I take off the gold watch that I wear every single day and flip it over. I press the small button to the compartment in the back, and it clicks open, spitting out a foldable key that my grandfather had specially designed eighty years ago. I walk toward the door in front of us, and I look up at her.

"This is the only entrance to the house that doesn't open by retina or fingerprints anymore," I tell her. "This was my grandfather's favorite part of the house. It was off limits to everyone except for him, me, and my brothers. Not even my cousins had access. When he was dying, he made us promise to keep it to ourselves. So we never updated the entry. My brothers and I each have the same watch with the key."

She smiles as I unlock it. Inside, I scoop her back up, carrying her up the swirling staircase that leads to the tower, which was really just a glorified study that my grandfather spent any free time he had in. His desk still sits in one corner, a huge sofa in another, and then in the adjoining room is a huge four-post bed.

"This is so cool," she whispers, looking around.

"Tyler is going to get our things from my suite and bring them up here. We'll hide up here tonight and be out first thing in the morning."

She nods, walking toward the large square window that faces the ocean, my grandfather's telescope still pointed at the sky.

"I'm sorry for what I said tonight," she says as she stares out over the water. I untie my tie, tugging it off, and walk over to her. I slink my arms around her and kiss her temple, then her jaw, then underneath her ear.

"You have nothing to be sorry for, Sawyer. I'm the one who should be apologizing to you. He tried to make you feel small, but the only thing he did was humiliate himself. I'm so...I'm so grateful that I get to even know you, let alone love you."

I spin her around to face me.

"He deserved every word you said. And if you hadn't given him a verbal beating, I'd have done it for you," I chuckle, and a little smile shows on her lips. I bend down to kiss them. "It's kinda hot, actually. The way you can bring a grown man to his knees." She smiles against my mouth.

"Oh, yeah?" she asks. I bite her lip gently, and her tongue dances across mine as we kiss softly, slowly.

"Yes," I say. I gently nudge her toward the French doors at the back of the room that open to a small balcony. It faces the water, away from the rest of the property. The perfect spot to feast. I open the doors and lead her outside, and she shivers when the cool breeze hits her skin. I know she's cold, but she won't be for long.

I slink down on my knees in front of her, reaching for the hem of her dress as it drags along the balcony floor.

"I have wanted to tear this off of you all night," I tell her.

"Don't you dare," she moans as she leans back against the railing. "This cost more than I make in a year at the mini-mart."

I smile as I look up at her, then I slide my hands up her legs slowly, raising the fabric up her creamy skin that's glowing in the moonlight.

"Do you know how sexy that was tonight, Sawyer?" I tell her as I trace soft kisses up from her knees to her upper thighs. "Do you know how badly I wanted to take you right there in that hall? How badly I wanted to show everyone what you do to me?"

"What do I do to you, Julian?" she breathes. I smile as I slide my hands up to her ass, my eyes widening when I realize she's got no panties on.

"You make me ravenous," I say, and then I dip my head under the fabric, hoisting her up by her thighs. She leans back on the railing, clutching onto it as I dive in, tongue first. I lick her slit up and down, tasting every drop she has ready for me, urging more. I suction my mouth against her clit, massaging it with my tongue while it swirls in my mouth, and she writhes against the stone behind her. I feel her hand clutch my hair, and I plunge two fingers inside her pussy while I eat her.

"Christ Almighty," she pants. "Julian, I—"

She can't finish her sentence, and I take that as my cue to continue driving her out of her fucking mind. I fuck her with my tongue, in and out, while my fingers massage her, her legs draped over my shoulders.

"That's a good girl," I say between licks. "Take these fingers, baby. Fuck my hand."

"Oh, fuck," she moans.

"Mm-hmm," I say then dive in for another taste. "That's such a good girl. Come for me now, baby. Let go and come."

She grips my hair tighter as I plunge back into her pussy, sucking at the fastest rhythm I can until I feel her thighs clench around me. Then she drops back, her body going limp, and I slowly re-emerge from out of the dress.

She shudders as the aftershock rolls through her, and I smile as I lick her juices off my lips. God, she's my favorite fucking flavor.

"Dear God," she pants, and I chuckle as I scoop her up, carrying her back into the room. I stand her in front of me, unzipping the back of the dress and letting it pool at her feet.

"I need more," she says, her chest still heaving.

"Oh, baby," I tell her, "we're not even close to being done."

I urge her toward the bed, pushing her down onto the mattress. I press her head gently toward it, and I pull her hips toward me so her perfect little ass is up in the air.

I spit on my hand and rub it on my cock, pumping myself twice before I grip her hips again. I slide into her, pounding in and out while she moans, her hands outstretched and gripping the sheets.

"Good girl," I tell her. "You're doing so good, baby. You're taking it so good, aren't you?"

"Mm-hmm," she says. I move faster, fucking her like I'm afraid she's going to slip away, and then when I'm close, I lean forward, pulling her up to me. I rub my fingers over her clit slowly while I pound into her, and she wraps her arm around me, tugging on my hair as little cries escape from her lips.

"Come all over this dick," I tell her. "Come for me, sweet girl. Come for Daddy."

I feel her start to tremble in my arm, and then I let myself go, exploding inside of her as she lets out a scream and falls forward. I catch her, laying her down gently as I slide out of her and collapse next to her on the bed. We catch our breath for a moment, and I rub her head and kiss her cheek. I slide off the bed and grab a towel from the bathroom, cleaning her up and dabbing at the wet spot on the bed.

"Was that me or you?" she asks sheepishly.

"I think that's a beautiful combo of both of us, honey," I tell her as I tuck her into me and pull the covers up around us.

SAWYER

The next morning, I move my arms and legs around the bed slowly, but I don't feel him. I sit up, rubbing my eyes, and I see him moving around the study, putting our things in our bags.

"Morning, baby," he says, walking over to me and kissing me on the forehead. "I left an outfit out for you. Get dressed. We gotta get out of here."

Before I can say anything, he's throwing the bags over his shoulders and walking down the stairs. I'm up and dressed before he's back up, and I take a mental picture of what the tower feels like. Of what it looks like. Of what being in this room that was so sacred to him felt like.

"Ready?" he asks from the top of the stairs. I nod, and he smiles and takes my hand. Tyler is outside at the door of the Escalade, which he's pulled up to the private driveway just outside the tower.

"Why are we rushing? Do you not want to say goodbye?" I ask as we climb inside. Julian smiles.

"Nah," he says. "I'll wave from the car."

As we drive away, I notice that we're getting on the highway in the direction of the airport. I raise an eyebrow.

"Where are we going?"

He doesn't answer. He just strokes the back of my hand and smiles. After a little while, we pull into the private driveway we pulled into when we dropped my mom off at his jet a few weeks ago.

"Julian, what are we doing?" I ask. The element of surprise is exciting, but I'm also too Type A for this. I have a schedule. Tyler parks a few yards back from the steps of the jet and gets out, unloading our bags. Julian unbuckles me then gets out, walks around the car, and opens my door. "Julian!" I say. "Tell me what is going on here."

Finally, he turns to me.

"We're going to Seattle," he says. "Short of blind-folding you, I wasn't sure how else to pull off the surprise besides just bringing you to the jet."

I feel my stomach flip.

"But...I...my flight...."

"I had Nat cancel it. We will get you your refund. I thought...I thought we could spend a few extra days with your mom."

I swallow.

"'We'?"

"You spent the evening with my family. I thought

maybe we could spend some time with yours. If you don't want me to go, though, I promise, I understand. I'll fly with you just to spend some time with you, and then I'll get a hotel. I just wanted you to get a little more time with her."

I feel my stomach flip again, and a knot forms in my throat.

"Julian...I...this is too much. This is..."

He takes a step toward me.

"I need you to trust me when I say that I will never be able to repay you all that you have given me."

I think for a minute.

"This is *so* nice. But I'm supposed to work two shifts before I fly out at the end of the week, and—"

He sighs, taking my hands in his.

"That's the other thing I wanted to talk to you about," he says. "Please don't take this as me being controlling or me trying to do anything but make your life easier. I want you to quit."

My eyebrows raise.

"Wh...what?"

"Just...hear me out, okay? I figured out how much you make hourly there. And then how much you would make if you worked five days a week, like you have been, for the rest of the semester. I deposited that much, plus an extra month's worth, knowing you'd probably stay for a few weeks after graduation, into your bank account last night."

My eyes widen again.

"You did what?" I ask. I'm overwhelmed with

conflicting emotions of both relief and feeling unsettled.

"I'm sorry. If you really don't want it, you can take it out. I just... You work so hard, baby. Between your classes starting back up, the mini-mart, and everything you've been through these last few months...I just want you to have a little break. You should get a break like every other student. You should get to spend time with your mom. I promise I didn't go overboard. It's just what you would have had if you had kept working."

"Julian, I don't..."

"You will never owe me. You can never owe someone who loves you anything, Sawyer." My eyes lock with his. "Just think about it, okay?"

I nod. I stare at him, his brownish-gray locks blowing in the wind, his perfectly imperfect nose, those big brown eyes that swallow me whole.

He does make me feel loved. And he does it really fucking well. I take a step toward him and take his hands again.

"I want to go to Seattle now," I say, "and I really want you to come with me to my mom's."

He smiles down at me as I throw my arms around his waist, burying myself into him.

ONCE WE'RE on the jet, I curl up next to him.

"Does all love feel this good?" I ask him.

He wraps an arm around me, pulling me into him

tight. He tucks a stray strand of hair behind my ear and stares down at me, his thumb stroking my cheek.

"I don't know," he says, "because I don't think I have ever known love until you."

* * *

WE LAND A FEW HOURS LATER, and I am giddy about getting to my mom. She doesn't know I'm coming in yet, which makes it even sweeter. And she definitely doesn't know that Julian will be with me, which makes it all the more exciting.

I'm not nervous about telling her. She has never been anything but supportive. Cautious, yes. But always supportive. My only fear is how my being with him might change her life. But that's a worry for another day. Today, I'm just going to bask in being with my two favorite human beings in my favorite city in the world.

Julian has a car waiting for us in the airfield, and Russ and Tyler are both with us. Russ drives, and Tyler sits shotgun as we make our way out and toward the city. I look out the window, soaking in the familiar skyline that's always given me so much peace. It's funny, though, because I don't feel that same sense of overwhelming relief I normally do being here. Like it's my sanctuary. Being with my mom, that will heal things in me that I didn't know were broken. But I've found peace in other places.

I instruct Tyler where to go to get to the little

neighborhood on the outskirts of downtown where the diner my mom works at is, perched on the corner. I see her car in the lot, and my stomach flips. We pull up, and suddenly, I feel nervous. I've never felt like Julian was judging me, but I don't want my mom to feel like she's being judged either.

But it's too late to turn back now, because we're parked, and Tyler is opening up my door. I turn back to Julian.

"Aren't you coming?" I ask. He shrugs.

"That's up to you, sweetheart," he says. "We can ease our way in, if you want."

But I think about the way he swept me through the door at Bedell House. How tightly he held my hand. How he showed them—and me—who I was to him. I smile and take his hand, bringing it to my lips.

"Come on," I tell him. He smiles at me as we both scoot out of the car. Tyler takes the front while Russ takes the rear, leading us into the diner. Luckily, it's eleven a.m. Seattle time, and no one is inside but the regulars and Randy, the owner.

He's the sweet old man who gave my very-pregnant teen mother a job. Who let her keep it while she had me, and who delivered home-cooked meals to her from his wife after I was born. He and his wife, Beth, are family.

"Morning," Randy calls from behind the counter without looking over to see who it is.

"Hi, Randy," I say, and he turns to us. His eyes widen when he sees me, and he scoots out from behind the counter, making his way to me with big, open arms. His belly has gotten rounder over the years, but he still looks like he always has. He wraps me up in a hug.

"Baby girl!" he says. "It is *so* good to see this face! Does your mama know you're here? She's in back."

I smile and hug him tight, shaking my head.

"I came in early to surprise her," I say. Then I remember Julian. I turn and grab him, pulling him forward. "*We* came in early. This is my boyfriend, Julian."

Julian sticks out a hand, and Randy eyes him up and down, shaking his hand enthusiastically. I'm sure he's going through all the questions: How old is he? Why do I recognize his face?

But before I can add anything else, the kitchen door swings open, and my mom walks out with a tray of food over her shoulder. She spins around, her eyes landing on us, and Randy rushes to her to rescue the tray before she drops it. It takes her a moment to process us standing there, but when she does, she screams and throws her hands up, running around the counter to us. She pulls me in, and I instantly feel home. I feel my body and mind ease as I wrap my arms around her tight.

"Hi, Mama," I say as we come apart.

"What are you doing here? I thought you weren't coming in till Thursday!" she says. Then she turns to Julian. "And Julian! It's so good to see you again! What...what brings you to Seattle?"

I clear my throat then reach back and take his hand in mine. I lift my eyes back to my mom, and her eyes are like saucers. She smiles, but I know her. I know she is the one with a million questions now. Julian reaches his free hand out and puts it on her shoulder.

"It's so good to see you, Emily," he says, then he bends down to me. "Tyler and I are going to go out to the car, sweetheart, and let you and your mom see each other for a few. Russ will hang in here with you. We'll be outside whenever you're ready."

I nod. He can read me like a book. He slips back out the door, and then I turn back to my mom. She takes my hand, leading me to the booth at the very back corner—the same one I used to sit and do my home-work in after school, waiting for her to get off. We scoot in opposite each other, and she just stares at me, holding my hands across the table.

"What's happening, baby?" she asks. I take a deep breath.

"He surprised me and flew me out here early so I could spend more time with you," I tell her. She tilts her head slightly, waiting for more. "Mom...we're... together."

I hold my breath, waiting to let it all sink in.

"Together?" she asks. "Like...you're dating?"

SAWYER

I nod.

"Yeah, Ma," I say.

"How...what happened?"

I swallow and shrug.

"I really don't know, Ma," I say. "We...we just spent a lot of time together after the shooting. He never stopped checking in on me, the apartment... I don't know. I just can't imagine him not being around now, ya know?"

She doesn't say much, her eyes just moving side to side while she takes it all in.

"He's a lot older than you, Sawyer," she says. It doesn't feel judgy. It just feels like she's going through it all in real time. I nod.

"Fifteen years," I say. She nods slowly, thinking it all through. We sit in silence for a moment before she finally speaks.

"I knew something was up when I was out there

for Thanksgiving. The way he looked at you...it was like...like you belonged to him."

I smile.

"I guess I did," I say. She takes in a long breath. "Are you okay, Ma?"

She looks at me again, sliding her hands across the table to mine again.

"Yes, baby," she says. "You are the most mature twenty-two-year-old in the world. You had to grow up so fast because of our circumstances. I trust your decision-making and your judgment. I've seen him be nothing but kind and do nothing but care for you. I just...his family...he comes with some baggage, babe. Are you ready for that?"

I nod.

"I actually went to a party at his family's estate last night," I tell her. She squeezes my hand, kicking her feet on the floor.

"You *what?!*" she squeals. "Oh, my *god!* You have to tell me everything."

I laugh.

"I will, Ma," I say. "But I just wanted to make sure *you* would be okay with it."

Her eyebrows knit together.

"Me? Why wouldn't I be?"

"Well, my being with him could affect *you*. Whenever it gets out, it could get a little nutty. Julian said that the press will dig into anyone and everything they can. I just...I want to make sure you're okay with it before—"

"Sawyer Jean Willis," she says, "this is *your* life. I have nothing for them to dig up. Let them. I love you, my girl. But it's your turn to think about *you*."

My eyes fill with tears as I nod.

"Thank you, Ma," I whisper.

"Well, let me see if Randy minds if—"

"Get outta here, girl. Go be with your baby!" Randy calls from around the corner, having likely eavesdropped on most of the conversation. We both chuckle and shake our heads. She takes off her apron, and we say our goodbyes as we walk out the door, Russ in tow. We walk to the Escalade, and Julian lowers the window.

"Not every day your daughter tells you she's dating an Everett," my mom says. Julian's eyes are big, like he's not sure how to respond. But finally, Mom smiles and puts her hand on his through the window. "I have felt so much relief since you came into her life, Julian. I knew she was in good hands when I couldn't be with her. I'm glad it's you."

He smiles and squeezes her hand.

"So am I," he laughs, "believe me."

"Follow us back to the apartment," my mom says. He looks at us.

"Are you sure you don't just want some time to—"

"Follow us!" she calls, pulling me to her car.

BACK AT OUR APARTMENT, I wait for Tyler to find a spot outside. Russ walks in with my mom, sweeping the building before we're allowed inside. The average person might not recognize Julian's face, but regardless, his net worth is still that of a country. When we get the all-clear, we walk inside and up the three flights of stairs. My mom is a neat freak, so I know the apartment will be spotless. And she lives for hosting, so I know she's in her element.

She's waving us inside, making Tyler and Russ glasses of iced tea as we get settled.

"Just put your things in Sawyer's room," she tells Julian, and we all freeze, staring. When she realizes, she scoffs. "What? You think I don't know you two have been shacking up in the city. She's no dummy, and I'm sure the Everetts don't just go around doing extracurricular activities without protection."

"Mom!" I choke out, but she just shrugs, and Julian bursts into a fit of laughter.

"Emily, I don't mean to put you out," he says when he finally composes himself. But she just puts a hand on her hip. She doesn't say anything else before he finally gets it. He throws his hands up in surrender. "If it's okay with you, I'd love to stay here." She smiles, he smiles, and I can't help but smile.

WE SPEND the next few days taking Julian to all our favorite spots downtown, getting our favorite coffee, and taking him to our favorite bookstore. We got out during off-times, and so far, we've stayed incognito. But I've suggested carry-out and delivery multiple times, giving him the break I know he craves from the world. When Christmas morning rolls around, I wake up to an empty bed. When I make my way out into the living room, I find my mom and Julian at the table, playing cards while they sip their coffee, laughing and talking. I wish I could freeze this moment, in my favorite place with my favorite people. The floor creaks beneath me, and they both look up.

"Merry Christmas, baby girl," my mom says with a warm smile. I walk over and kiss her forehead then sit on Julian's lap.

"Merry Christmas, baby," he whispers as he kisses my cheek. Then he nods his head toward the tree. "Think there's something over there for you."

I roll my eyes and shake my head as I steal his coffee and walk over to the tree. I divvy out gifts as they join me, noticing that there are a ton more than I had ordered for my mom. I look at him, but he won't make eye contact with me. I don't even know how he had time to do this or how he snuck them in here. But I fucking love him.

He got my mom clothes, a new watch, and unlimited air miles to New York to visit. He also reserved her a suite at the nicest hotel in Connecticut for my graduation this spring. I can tell how uncomfortable she is but how grateful at the same time. Then, he turns to me, handing me a small box. I rip off the wrapping and open the box, staring down at the ornament that I loved from that shop in Bendmere a few months ago. I look up at him and smile.

"You sneaky sneak," I say, pulling it out of the box and leaning over to hang it on the tree. But as I go to close the box, I notice something else gleaming in the light. And then I see it: the tiny silver key that sits on a chain. My eyes grow wide.

"Is...is this..."

"That was my grandfather's key to the tower," he says. "He told me to keep it until I found it the right home. And I did."

I look up at him, my eyes filling with tears. I pluck it from the box, putting it on and clutching it in my hand. I'm at a loss for words, so I just crawl over to him, kissing him and nestling into him. I play with the key, dangling it across my fingers.

I think he might really love me.

We spend the rest of the day in our pajamas, drinking coffee and hot chocolate, eating the gourmet dinner Mom made us, and watching *The Family Stone*, just as my mom and I do every single Christmas. We don't have heirlooms or towers, but we have traditions. And we have quality time. And enough love to go around.

That night, in my childhood bedroom, Julian and I make love to the light of the moon through the window. He has to fly home tomorrow for work, but another Everett jet will be in the area at the end of break that will bring me back to New York.

I know it's only a few weeks, and he plans to visit a few times, but my heart already hurts.

I'm no good at being without him anymore.

. . .

My mom had an early morning shift at the diner, and although Julian wanted me to sleep in, I insisted on riding with him to the airport. I dropped my mom off at her shift then met them on the airstrip.

I pull the car up behind the SUV they rented and hop out. He's waiting for me on the tarmac, looking like a whole damn snack leaned up against it.

I realize I look ridiculous, but I run to him, and he catches me with open arms and a smile. He kisses me, lifting me off the ground, and then I bury myself in his neck.

"I know this is clingy as hell, but I really don't want you to go," I say. He chuckles, squeezing me tighter.

"If you're clingy, then I'm obsessed, because I almost canceled all my meetings this morning."

I kiss his neck and cheek, and he sets me down.

"Enjoy your time with your mom," he says. "But just know that when you get back, you're all mine." I smile and kiss him one last time. "I love you, Sawyer."

"I love you," I tell him as he kisses my forehead one more time before walking to the plane. He turns at the bottom of the stairs.

"Let me know as soon as you get home," he says. I smile and salute him. I love having someone who looks out for me the way he does. Like I don't have to be the only one with my eyes on everything all the time. I blow him a kiss, and then he's off.

* * *

THE NEXT FEW days with my mom are amazing. Randy gave her the day off, and she didn't have to work at the coffee shop either. I hate how much she works. I hate that she spends her days serving others without anyone to ever serve her. I want her to rest. I want her to live life, not work through it. And one day, I'm going to make sure that's exactly what happens.

We go to the park together, drive around the suburbs, looking at Christmas lights, and watch our favorite movies. We look through old pictures, clean out some old things in the apartment, and eat all our favorite foods. On my last night, we lie in her bed, binge-watching old *Grey's Anatomy* episodes while we each enjoy a pint of ice cream.

"Mom?" I say, licking my spoon and setting it down on the nightstand.

"Hmm?"

"He wants me to quit my job," I say. It's been on my mind since we left New York, and I've been struggling with what to do about it. She looks at me then sets her own ice cream down.

"He what?"

I sigh.

"He wants me to quit my job. He says I've been working so much that I'm not enjoying my last semester. And that after everything I've been through this year, I deserve the break. He gave me the same amount of money that I would make working the same number of shifts each week at the mini-mart, plus a little extra. It's already in my account," I say. She stares at me intently.

"Okay," she says with a slight pause. "And how do you feel about that?"

I shrug.

"I don't know," I say honestly. "I mean, you always taught me not to depend on anyone financially, especially a man. But on the other hand, man, it would be really nice not to work that job. Just to chill for a little bit before I join the real world. I don't know...what do you think?"

She thinks for a minute.

"I hear you, baby," she says. "But honey, I never depended on anyone because I didn't have the option to. As a woman, I want nothing more than for you to be able to have that freedom financially. But honey, there is plenty of time for that. This man...he loves you. And as your mom, selfishly, it makes me ecstatic. He's right. You deserve it. And if I could give you the same thing, I would a million times over. Honey, our life has been *hard*. And a few months ago, yours got even harder. I love how independent you are, baby. But please don't make the mistake of thinking you don't deserve love and the things that come with it."

I nod.

"I know. You're right," I say. "I just don't want to take advantage of him. I don't want him to think I'm with him for that."

She smiles.

"Baby, if I know you, I know you've never asked that man for a single thing as long as you've known him. Am I right?" I nod. "Exactly. Let him love you. And love him back."

I smile and snuggle up next to her.

That ship has certainly sailed.

THE LAST MORNING of break at home with my mom, I wake up before my alarm, my stomach in knots. I don't want to leave my mom, but I am desperate for him. My body aches, and I haven't stopped twirling the key around my neck. I send him a text when I get up.

Packing up now. I can't wait to see you, I send.

An hour goes by, but no response. I know he's been in all-day meetings this week, so I don't read too much into it while I get my things together. Mom drives me to the airport, and we follow Russ's instructions and use the badges they left us to get onto the private tarmac. I send off another text.

At the airport, I send off. *About to board.*

Nothing.

My Spidey-senses are tingling. I turn to my mom.

"I miss you already," I tell her. "I can't wait to see you again."

She pulls me in for a long hug.

"I'll cash in those miles from Julian soon," she says as she squeezes me. "Let's pick a date when you're back."

I nod.

"I love you, Ma," I say. She kisses my cheeks a million times.

"I love you, sweetie."

She gets out when I do, standing at her car and watching the whole way as I climb the stairs to the plane. She waves until the plane door closes, and I blow her one final kiss from the window.

I look down at my phone again.

About to take off. I love you.

I wait until lift off.

Still nothing.

DESPITE MY INCREASING ANXIETY, I doze off during the flight. I wake up as we're starting our descent, checking my phone again. Nothing. Finally, I give in to my anxiety, and as the wheels touch down, I call him.

It rings, and rings, and rings.

Then it goes to his voicemail.

I grab my bag and rush off the plane, hustling across the tarmac where Tyler is waiting at the Escalade. But when he opens the door, I realize that Julian isn't with him. I turn to Tyler before I get in.

"Where is Julian?" I ask. He looks uncomfortable, and he clears his throat.

"I'm not sure, ma'am," he says.

Ma'am?

"Tyler," I say sternly, "what is going on? Is he okay?"

He clears his throat again.

"He's safe, Sawyer. I'm afraid I can't say much more than that," he says, ushering me into the car. I swallow as I climb inside.

What the fuck is going on?

I tap my foot against the floor of the car the entire drive back to my apartment. As we pull up, I look at Tyler through the rearview mirror.

"Can you take me to the penthouse?" I ask. Tyler stares down at his hands on the steering wheel for a minute.

"Sorry, Sawyer," he says. "There's a... He's not there. He's at the office. I was just told to bring you back here."

I swallow. *At the office?*

He helps me out, grabbing my bag from the backseat. But before he can take another step, I take it from him.

"I got it from here," I say. "Thank you."

I rush up the three flights to my apartment, letting myself in and locking the door before Tyler can catch me to do the sweep. I don't give a fuck right now, though. My heart is pounding in my chest, and I can't get a hold of the one person who can calm me back down.

I send him one more desperate text.

What the fuck is going on, Julian? Call me. Please.

I sit down on the couch, looking out over the water like I always do. But right now, I feel anything but peace.

SAWYER

*a*n entire week passes with absolutely no contact from Julian. I've never been ghosted before, but let me tell you, it ain't the most fun I've ever had. I'm pretty sure I've lost a few pounds. Classes start back up next week, and I have no idea how I'm going to function. I can't eat, my sleep has been horrible, and my focus is for shit. I'm tempted to ask for my job at the mini-mart back just to keep myself busy. But I'm not sure I could handle having to be productive in any capacity right now. After I sent that last Hail Mary text, I decided to stop reaching out. I know my mom can sense something is up, but I haven't told her anything.

The whiplash from realizing you're in love with someone to having them abandon you is one I don't care to experience again. I force a bowl of soup down then curl up on the couch. I turn on *Cheers*, and I feel the tears prick in my eyes. And like I've done for the last seven days, I let them fall until I drift off to sleep.

I wake up the next morning to the couch vibrating. I blink my eyes a few times, holding the phone up to my face.

102 missed notifications.

Calls from my mom.

Texts from friends from school.

Email from one of my professors.

I play one of my mom's voicemails.

"Baby, call me, please," she says, *"I need to make sure you're okay. How did this happen?"*

Yoooooo, JULIAN EVERETT?! WHATTTTT, a text from Maddie reads.

Another text has a link to an article. I click it, and my stomach somersaults.

Julian Everett Dating Carrington University Student, the headline reads.

Oh, fuck.

Julian Everett, eldest son of Cato Everett, was seen cozying up to Carrington student Sawyer Willis at a private party at Bedell House a few weeks back. Drone footage caught the two on the grounds during what sources say was the birthday party of Julian's stepmother, Angelina.

Fuck. Fuck, fuck, fuckety fuck.

The photo is blurry, but it's clear enough to make out me over Julian's shoulder as he carried me through the garden.

How did they know it was me?

"I've had a few classes with Sawyer," says her class-mate, Elle Richards. "She's a great girl. I'm so happy that she's happy."

Elle Richards? I don't even know an Elle Richards.

My heart is thudding in my chest, and I can feel the bile building up.

What do I do?

But there's no one to ask.

Because he's not here.

I take a breath and call my mom.

"Baby, hi," she says. I can hear the plates clanking in the background, and I know she's at the diner. "Are you alright? What's going on?"

I pause for a minute. As much as I'd love to fall apart right now, I can't. Because she'll get on a plane. She'll fly out here the second she knows I need her. She'll give up her shifts and have to work doubles when she gets back to make up for it.

I swallow back the lump in my throat.

"Hey, Ma," I say, keeping my voice as light and airy as possible. "We're not sure how it got out yet, but I just wanted you to know I'm okay. We knew this would happen eventually. Just, uh...just keep an eye out around you. Eventually, they'll find you too," I tell her.

"Jeez, baby, this is a lot," she says. "Don't you worry about me. Are *you* okay?"

I quickly brush her off, desperate to get off the phone.

"Yes, yes," I say. "Really, I'm fine. The Everetts

know how to handle this, luckily. I'll let you know how it's all going. I promise."

She sighs on the other line.

"Maybe I should come out there," she says.

"No, Ma," I say. "No. Really, I'm fine. We're fine," I lie.

"Alright," she concedes. "But please call me if anything changes. Keep me posted."

"Okay, Ma. I love you. Bye."

My fight-or-flight is activated.

And right now, flight is winning.

I can't go anywhere because I don't know where is "safe."

I can't call anyone because I don't have anyone who can help me navigate this.

So instead, I hole up in my apartment.

A FEW MORE DAYS PASS, and I've been a recluse to the world. The only person I've answered is my mom, and that's only to keep up the charade that everything is fine. I've deleted all my social media and so far have succeeded in keeping the world at bay. But today, classes start again, and it's time to face the music.

It would be a lot less complicated if the world found out I was dating a billionaire while I was actually in touch with him. Now, I have no idea what the fuck is happening.

But instead of letting him win, I have managed to put on real clothes, brush my teeth, and make my way to campus. It's been a few more days since the news broke, so maybe it's old news.

I park my bike in the same bike rack I always have, and as I step foot up onto the red brick walkway, a chill goes down my spine. This corner of campus will always hold so much weight. Despite the new pavers they put down, my eyes will always see the blood spatters and hear the screams. I shake my head and keep walking, rounding the corner onto the main quad.

I try not to make eye contact with anyone, until I am stopped by the flash of a camera in my face. Then another, then another. And then twenty or so students surround me. And then twenty or so more. And suddenly, I can't breathe.

"Miss Willis, how long have you been dating Julian Everett?" a reporter asks, shoving a microphone in my face.

"We're here on the Carrington campus, where Sawyer Willis, a student here who is rumored to be dating Julian Everett of the Everett family, has just arrived," I hear another say.

"Sawyer, hey, let me get a picture!" I hear someone else say.

I can't breathe. I push to move past them, but I can't break free.

And then I feel a hand grab my arm. And then another hand grabs my other arm. Tyler on my right, Russ on my left. Tyler tucks me under his arm while Russ pushes through the crowd. I bury myself into

Tyler as they rush me to the Escalade, thrusting me inside and peeling out of the parking lot.

I stare out the window at the mob we just escaped when I hear his voice.

"Sawyer," he says.

JULIAN

 y heart fucking *aches*. I tried to get out of the car to get to her, but Russ reminded me that that would put her in more danger.

So I sat here like a fucking schmuck while they rescued her. And now she's here with me, and the ache is real. These last few weeks have been fucking torture. And if she hadn't gone back to campus today, I would have continued not contacting her. And I would have been a fucking miserable shell of a man like I have been.

"Sawyer," I say, and her eyes grow wide. She looks scared. She looks confused. And we stare at each other for a moment before she bursts into tears. I lunge for her, pulling her into me and holding her tight. She tries to push me off for a second, but then she resigns, going limp against me as I cradle her.

"Shh," I tell her. "You're safe. It's okay."

Finally, she composes herself, then she pushes away.

"What the fuck is going on?" she finally says.

I take in a long breath.

"Sawyer, I..."

"No. I want to get out," she says. "Russ, pull over, please."

"Sawyer, we're not—"

"Pull over, Russ. I want to get out," she says.

He looks at me through the rearview mirror, and I nod. He drives another minute or two until we get to a little park and pulls in. He parks, and then he and Tyler get out to give us privacy.

"Can we talk before you get out?" I ask her. "Please, Sawyer. Let me explain."

She scoots as far away from me as possible, crossing her arms over her chest defensively.

"Speak," she says. "Please, explain why you tell me you're in love with me one day and completely abandon me the next."

I swallow.

Abandon.

That's what I did.

It had to be done, but it doesn't mean it was anything less than abandonment. And I hate myself for it. I pause for a minute, and it enrages her all over again.

"Speak, Julian, or I'm getting out now. Tell me what was so important that you couldn't tell me. Tell me what made you spend fucking Christmas with my *mother* then leave me. God, you know what? I can't fucking believe how dumb I was. Angelina was right."

My eyes narrow.

"Whoa, whoa, whoa," I say. "Angelina was right about what?"

"At your dad's party," she says. "She told me we were just stops along the way for you. That our time with the Everett family wouldn't be long. And she was fucking right, wasn't she? God dammit. You know, I really have no one to blame but myself. You know the craziest part? You didn't even have the decency to check in when the news broke. You just *left* me."

I swallow.

God, I want to hold her.

"Sawyer," I say, "Everett Enterprises...we're in trouble."

She stares at me, wide-eyed, her jaw tight.

"What...what does that mean?"

I sigh.

"I'll tell you everything, but can we please go home first? Please. Just give me a chance to explain. I know I hurt you. I know I left you. You have every right to be upset. But please believe me when I tell you that I thought it was the only way to save you from something much worse. Please."

We sit in silence for a moment, then she finally nods.

"Okay."

A little while later, we're back in the penthouse, and I lead her into my study.

She sits down in the chair on the opposite side of the desk, and I pull up my email.

"The day I got back from Seattle, I got this email in my inbox," I say, turning the monitor around to her.

I watch as she reads it, her eyes growing wider with each sentence.

MR. EVERETT,

ENCLOSED PLEASE FIND *a detailed statement from a source who says that she was employed by your father from 2021-2023 and was repeatedly sexually harassed. The source also claims that there are multiple additional victims and that they are also willing to make statements. I would like to meet with you to discuss these claims. Kindly respond by the end of the week. Otherwise, I will have to go to print with the information I have.*

THANK YOU,

WREN WRIGHT
   Business & News Managing Editor
   Manhattan Times

JULIAN

She looks up at me, eyes wide.

"Wha...what?"

I swallow. Then I get up and walk around to the other side of the desk, leaning against it so I'm directly in front of her.

"We reached out to her and asked her to hold on the story so we could buy ourselves more time. But in the meantime, my legal team has been working on things to see what steps we should take. I asked them about you," I say.

"About me?"

I nod.

"I have no clue how far this goes," I say, "but I know it's more than just these few women who came forward. And I know that it all links back to my dad. I don't know how long. I don't know the extent of what he did, but obviously, it's tied to the company, and the company is tied to me. And up until a few weeks ago, so were you. Legal suggested, for your protection, that I cut contact with you. If I get subpoenaed, they can go for my phone records, and I can't do that to you, Sawyer. I can't have you dragged down with this. It's bad enough that my brothers and I may have to pay for his mistakes. But I refuse to let this affect you too. Please believe me when I say that these last few weeks, leaving you like that...it was the hardest thing I've ever done. And if we're being honest, I would have kept it up. But when the news broke last week and with classes starting up today, we knew this could get rocky for you, and I wasn't going to let you be in danger. I will supply security for you for the rest of the semester. I've added your name to the lease of the apartment so that it looks like you're a regular tenant. But you and me... I cannot take you down with me. I love you too much for that. I won't..." I feel my voice cracking. Because if there was ever a time I needed someone, it's right now. And if there was ever someone I needed, it's her.

She stands from her chair, walking toward me and pulling me into her.

I wrap my arms around her, and *God,* I forgot how this feels. A part of me heals every time she touches me.

She tilts my head up so we're looking into each other's eyes.

"I love you, Julian," she says, "but you don't get to decide what's best for me. Only I get to decide that." She reaches for my hand and interlocks our fingers.

"I'm not going to leave you because of something you didn't even do. I'm staying right here with you. I'll do whatever I can to help you, but just know that I'm not scared. I'm not worried about hard things. Life is hard, Julian. But it's much harder without the people we love."

I smile up at her, stroking her cheek with my thumb.

"How did you get to be so wise?" I ask her. She smiles and shrugs.

"Old soul, I guess," she says. I feel the smile drop from my face.

"What about school? There is no way to keep you from being badgered about this day and night once everything breaks."

She shrugs again.

"I'll finish my credits online. It's only a semester."

I roll my lips as I think. I hate the thought of her sacrificing so much just for me.

"This is going to get really ugly, baby," I tell her. "There's going to be a lot of shit to go through."

She bends down and kisses my lips softly.

"Then we go through it together," she whispers. "And if you lose it all, I can teach you how to be a regular, boring old middle-class citizen. No sweat." She winks, and I laugh, pulling her down onto my lap.

"God, I missed you," I say as I kiss her again.

"Show me how much," she whispers against my lips, and I waste absolutely no time. I spring to my feet, grabbing her by the waist and spinning her around, laying her gently on my desk.

"Listen," I tell her, "before I make you scream my name, I want you to know something."

She smiles.

"Yes?"

"I'm going to marry you one day," I tell her. She laughs.

"Is that so?" she asks. I nod. "Deal. But I want a prenup."

It makes me laugh out loud, but her face is serious.

"I am dead serious," she says. "I want nothing but whatever I come into the marriage with. And you can keep your hands off my fortune too."

I smile down at her.

"You have a fortune?" I say.

"Nah, but someday, I might."

I smile and kiss her again.

"Deal."

WE FUCK like rabbits all over my office until we're a sweaty mess, panting on the leather couch that sticks to my bare ass when we're done. We shower off, make a bowl of popcorn, and climb into my bed while the sun sets over Manhattan, and she curls up against me as the next episode of *Cheers* starts.

We met the day she saved my life. And the truth is, she's been saving me every day since then. Everything I've ever known in my life is about to come crashing down, but with her here in my bed, it doesn't feel as doomed. It feels like I'll get through it. It feels like the world will still turn. If I never did anything but wake up next to her every day for the rest of my life, I'd know it was a life well lived, all because Sawyer Willis loved me.

EPILOGUE

JULIAN

*I*t's been a week since we had the discussion after we rescued her from campus. Since she told me she was all in. And God, I've never felt more fortunate in my entire charmed life. The reporter who reached out to me is being strangely easy to work with, but I'm not positive how long that will last. I spend half my time keeping the businesses running and making sure that my dad has no inkling that anything is off or that anyone is on to him.

I spend the other half with my private legal team, devising a plan and figuring out how to get to the bottom of all this. The thing is, I knew the moment I read the email that it wasn't a lie. I was never a witness to it; my father tends to keep me out of his private company affairs—no pun intended, and I never heard any rumblings of it. But the thing is, I know him. I know his nature. I've seen the way he discards people, how little he knows about the people who work for him—including his own sons—and how much he cares about how productive they are. When the world is moving toward flexibility and a work-life balance, he stands ten toes down, forcing a culture that he himself has never had to respond to.

I don't hate my father. Even through all of this, despite what I may find out about him, there's still a kid in me that adores him and holds on to the idea that one day he may turn out to be the man I always hoped he would.

But grown-up Julian knows the truth—that if I want a man like that in my life, then I'd have to become him.

I'm in my study at the penthouse, staring out over the city but not taking in any of it. I dial both my brothers from the burner phone Nat ordered for me when all of this happened. Sawyer gave them a tip that I was going to call.

They both pick up at the same time, and it's really good to see their faces. Keaton appears to be on a balcony, and Brooks is lying on a beach. I roll my eyes.

"Do you ever work?" I ask him. He laughs and shrugs.

"What's up, J?" Keaton asks, ignoring both of us. "Why are you calling us from this number? And why did Sawyer have to tell us?"

"I need you both to be somewhere private," I say. I see Keaton stand up immediately and move into his apartment. The expression on Brooks's face goes from his normal carefree to "oh shit" real quick when he sees Keaton moving. He stands up from the chaise and jogs across the beach. When his camera stops shaking, I see that he's in some fancy resort suite.

"I'm good," Keaton says.

"Me too," Brooks says. I sigh as I lean over the phone in my desk chair.

"Boys, we're in for it," I tell them. "And the only way out is if we're together, and we take down the king."

Keaton stares at me wide-eyed. He knows what I'm saying. Brooks is confused, and I sigh. This isn't how I wanted to try to convince him of what we wanted to do, but I don't have a choice. There's no slow rollout to this. He's either with us, or he's with my dad.

I tell them the story. I read them the email, and then I wait a beat.

"Fuck," Brooks says, rubbing his temple. "Do you think he did it?"

Keaton scoffs.

"Of course he fucking did it," he says. "He does whatever the fuck he wants."

"Fuck," Brooks says again.

"So what are you thinking, J?" Keaton asks.

"I think you both need to come to New York. Tomorrow," I say. "I'll have legal ready to meet with us. Looks like our post-Cato plans are going to need to be rolled out faster than we had initially thought, Keat."

Keat thinks for a moment, nodding.

"Let's do it," he says. "I'll be there tomorrow."

There's a silence on the other end, and we both wait to gauge Brooks's response.

"I'll be there too," he says. "I don't know what you guys are talking about. But I know that there's no one else in my life I trust more than you two bastards."

I smile faintly and nod.

"Tomorrow," I say. They both nod.

"Tomorrow," they say in unison.

I hit the red button and take in a deep breath, rubbing my temples. I hear a soft knock on my office door.

"Come in," I say. She does, prancing across the floor like a little doe. And God, does it do me good to lay eyes on her.

"I brought you some tea," she says. "You've been in here all day." She sets the mug down on my desk then climbs onto my lap and pulls my head into her chest. It's such a cathartic feeling when she holds me like this. Like, for a few short minutes, I don't have to be the brains of the operation, or the family coordinator, or the CEO. I can just breathe against her.

"I'm sorry, baby," I say, pulling off her to pull her down into a kiss. She smiles.

"Don't be sorry," she says. "Just drink."

I smile and nod, taking a sip of the perfectly brewed tea.

"Do you know that you are my entire sunshine?" I ask her. She tilts her head, a little smirk playing on her perfect lips.

T.D. COLBERT

"What do you mean?"

"I mean that everything for me points to you. My day can be...this," I say, motioning to my desk and all the mounds of paperwork, "but my axis still points to you. My direction is clear. You're the reward I get when I get through a day like these last ones. You are the fresh air when it feels like I can't breathe."

She smiles, leaning down so our lips are just centimeters apart.

"And you are my moon," she says. "Because when I feel like I'm starting to spin out of control, you pull me back."

"What a pair we make, then, huh?" I say. She shrugs and kisses me again. "I need to tell you something. But first, come with me."

I lift her off my lap and lead her out of my study, down the stairs, and to the elevator. I nod at Tyler, and he follows us in then opens the doors when we get to the car.

"Where are we going?" she asks, and I smile. I wonder if she ever gets tired of these surprise adventures. But this one is a doozy. I just shrug as I take her hand, stroking the back of it with my thumb. After a few minutes, she knows, and I love how familiar she's becoming with all things Everett. "Bedell House?"

I smile and shrug again.

The ride is peaceful, mostly quiet. A few things here and there, but she doesn't ask any questions because she knows now that I'm a hard nut to crack. Finally, Tyler pulls us in and up the long driveway then turns right once we're on property and pulls around to the west tower. He stops and helps her out.

"What are we doing here?" she asks. I smile.

"Where's your key?" I ask her. She pulls the chain out from her shirt, lifting it off over her head. I use it to open the door then lead her up the stairs. When we get inside, I pull her into the room, and she looks around, confused until she sees a black velvet box on the windowsill.

Her eyes widen as she stares at it.

I lead her to it, picking it up and spinning toward her.

"Sawyer Jean, I'm in love with you," I tell her. "This next part of our lives might get a little rocky, but I know we will figure it out because I have you. I'm not proposing tonight," I tell her. And her eyes bounce from the box, to me, back to the box. Her eyebrows knit together in confusion. I take her hand. "I want to do that when the potential downfall of my family legacy isn't hanging over me. I want to do it when our lives aren't consumed with other things. But tonight, I want to promise something to you. And I'm asking for you to promise me something in return."

"Okay..." she says. I open the box, and inside sits a thin band with teeny, tiny diamonds around it.

"This band was my great-grandmother's. This was all my great-grandfather could afford before he struck the oil. He gave it to me on my twenty-first birthday. He told me to hold onto it until I found the woman who'd wear it. The woman who'd love me even if we never struck oil, just like she did for him. It's been in my safe ever since...until today."

She stares at it, her eyes filling with tears.

"So, you never gave it to—"

"Nope. Not even then. I guess I just knew, deep down. But then I met you, and I realized, Sawyer, the real oil strike was when I found you."

She blinks, the tears streaming down her face.

"So, what's the promise?" she asks. I slip the ring out of the box and take her hand.

"Just to love me and stand with me while I dismantle everything in my life and figure out how to put it all back together again. And then when I do, promise to say *yes* when I beg you to be my wife. Promise you'll consider spending this crazy life with me. Promise that if you ever decide you want to start a family, it's with me."

She smiles as I slide the ring on her finger.

"I promise," she says.

I kiss her long and hard before I pull away.

"Oh, and there's one more thing," I say with a smile as the tower door swings open...

BONUS EPILOGUE

Want one more piece of Sawyer and Julian's story?

Get it here: https://bit.ly/oldmoneybonus

Pre-order book two in the series, HUSH MONEY, to find out what happens next for the Everett brothers and their leading ladies!

ABOUT THE AUTHOR

T.D. Colbert is a romance and women's fiction author. When she's not chasing her family, she's probably under her favorite blanket, either reading a book or writing one. She lives in Maryland, where she was born and raised. For more information, visit www. tdcolbert.com.

Follow T.D. on TikTok, Instagram and Twitter, @taydanaewrites, and on Facebook, Author T.D. Colbert, for information on upcoming books!

Are you a blogger or a reader who wants in on some secret stuff? Sign up for my newsletter, and join **TDC's VIPs** - T.D.'s reader group on Facebook for exclusive information on her next books, early cover reveals, giveaways, and more!

www.ingramcontent.com/pod-product-compliance
Lightning Source LLC
Chambersburg PA
CBHW021233250626
47155CB00008B/2993